small things

Mel Tregonning

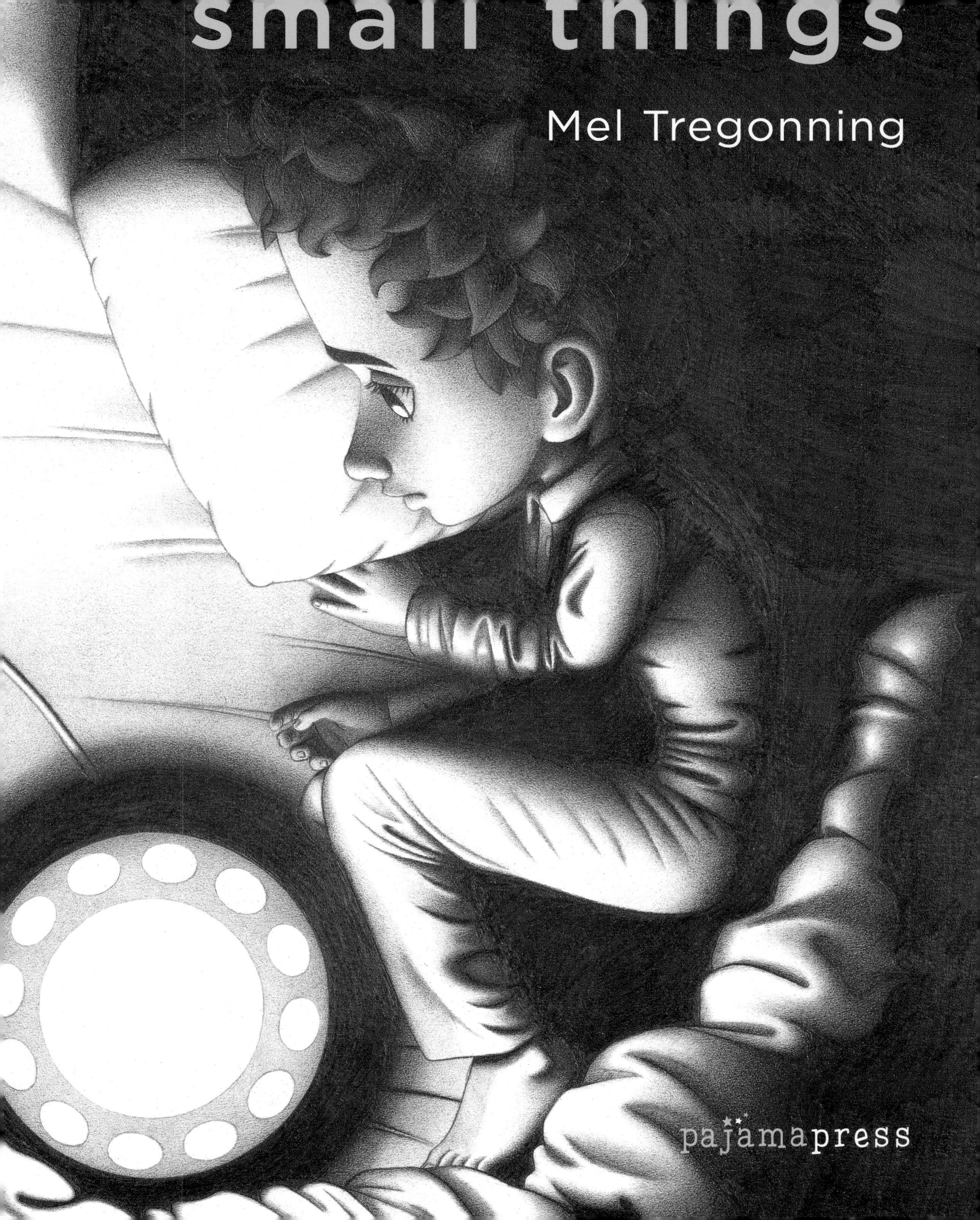

pajamapress

First published in Canada and the United States in 2018

This edition copyright © 2018 Pajama Press Inc.
Originally published by Allen & Unwin: Crow's Nest, New South Wales, Australia, 2016
Thanks to Shaun Tan for additional artwork direction and assistance
Text and illustration copyright © 2016 Estate of Mel R. Tregonning

10 9 8 7 6 5 4 3 2 1

www.pajamapress.ca   info@pajamapress.ca

Canada Council   Conseil des arts
for the Arts   du Canada

ONTARIO ARTS COUNCIL
CONSEIL DES ARTS DE L'ONTARIO
an Ontario government agency
un organisme du gouvernement de l'Ontario

Canada

The publisher gratefully acknowledges the support of the Canada Council for the Arts and the Ontario Arts Council for its publishing program. We acknowledge the financial support of the Government of Canada through the Canada Book Fund (CBF) for our publishing activities.

Library and Archives Canada Cataloguing in Publication

Tregonning, Mel, 1983-2014, author, illustrator   Small things / Mel Tregonning.
Previously published: Allen & Unwin Children's Books, 2016. ISBN 978-1-77278-042-0 (hardcover)
        1. Stories without words. 2. Graphic novels I. Title.
PZ7.7.T74Sm 2018   j741.5'994   C2017-906953-5

Publisher Cataloging-in-Publication Data (U.S.)

Names: Tregonning, Mel, author, illustrator.
Title: Small things / Mel Tregonning.
Description: Toronto, Ontario Canada : Pajama Press, 2018. | Originally published by Allen & Unwin, Australia, 2016. | Summary: "In a wordless graphic picture book, a young boy's struggle with anxiety is represented by swarms of tiny creatures that follow and gnaw away at him. As his schoolwork and social interactions suffer, he feels more alone and out of control. He ultimately begins to overcome his isolation when he opens up to his sister and learns he is not the only one beset with worries"— Provided by publisher.
Identifiers: ISBN 978-1-77278-042-0 (hardcover)
Subjects: LCSH: Depression, Mental – Juvenile fiction. | Loneliness – Juvenile fiction. | Stories without words. | BISAC: JUVENILE FICTION / Social Themes / Depression & Mental Illness. | JUVENILE FICTION / Comics & Graphic Novels / General.
Classification: LCC PZ7.T744Sm |DDC [Fic] – dc23

Original art created with graphite on paper
Cover and text: based on original design by Sandra Nobes

Manufactured by Friesens
Printed in Canada

Pajama Press Inc.
181 Carlaw Ave. Suite 207 Toronto, Ontario Canada, M4M 2S1

Distributed in Canada by UTP Distribution
5201 Dufferin Street Toronto, Ontario Canada, M3H 5T8

Distributed in the U.S. by Ingram Publisher Services
1 Ingram Blvd. La Vergne, TN 37086, USA

Mel,
We dedicate this book to you, we hope you can now rest.
Your dream became our dream, we have all worked so hard.
We have never loved you more and felt as proud as we do now.
Violet, Phil, Mum & Dad

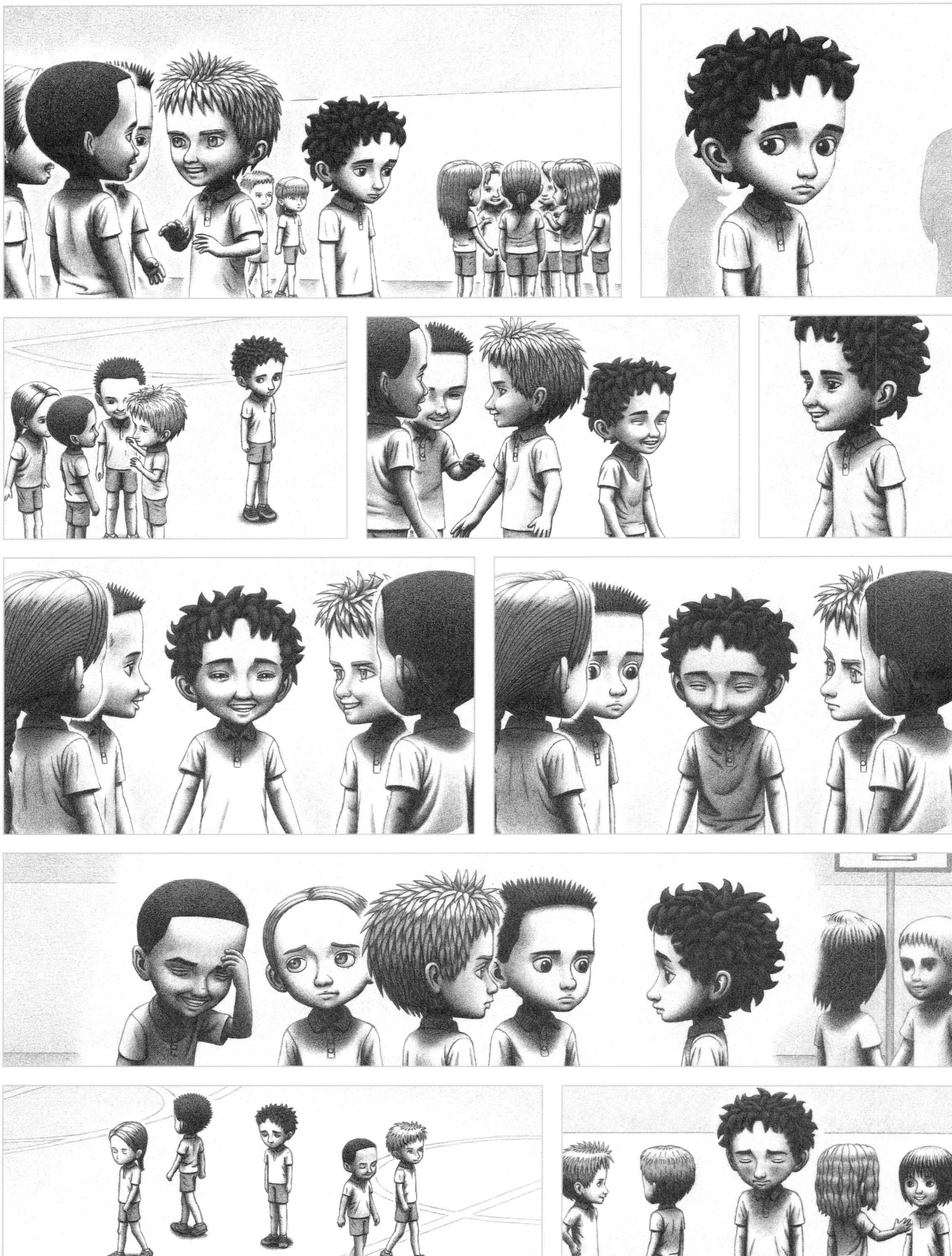

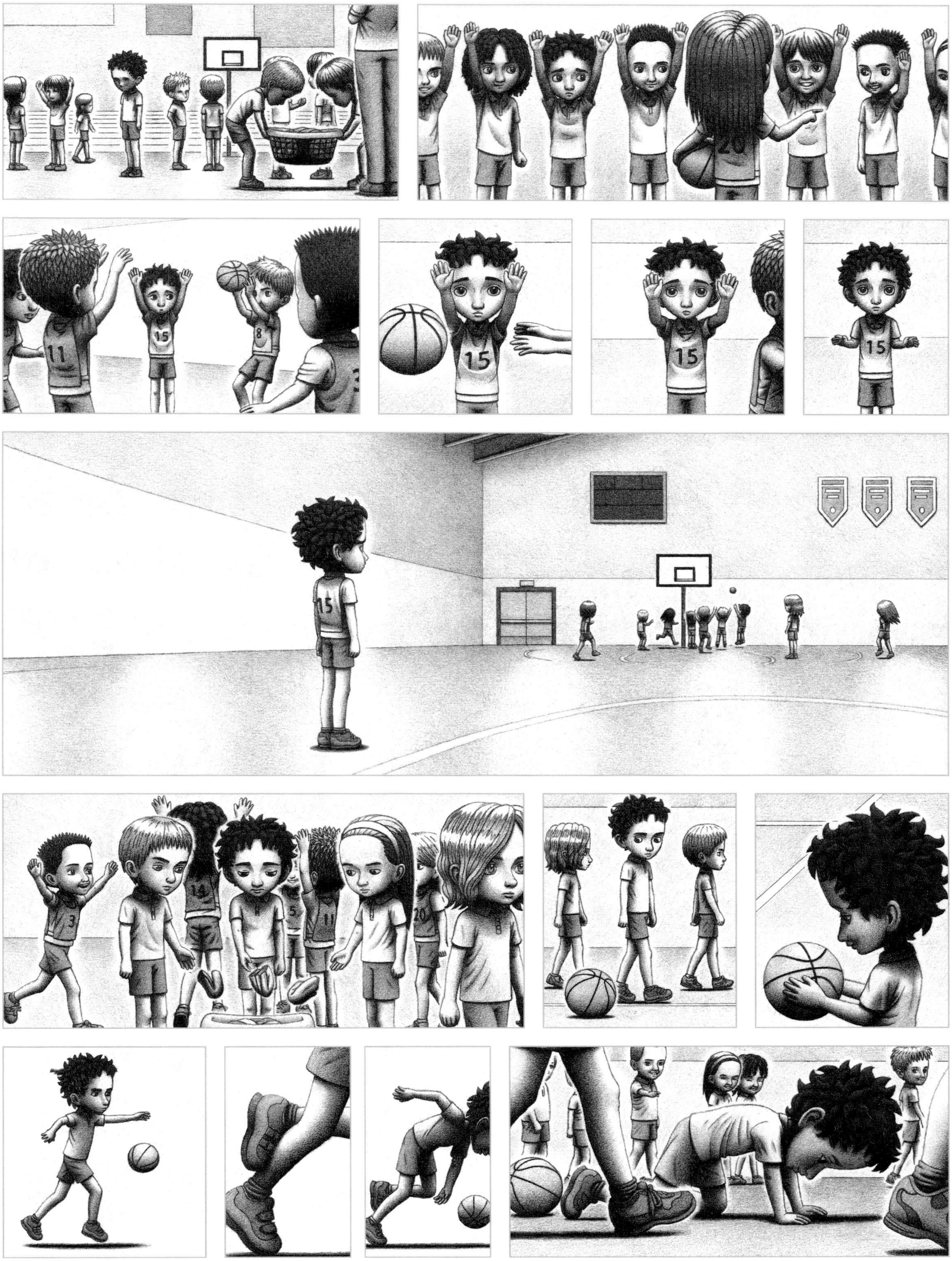

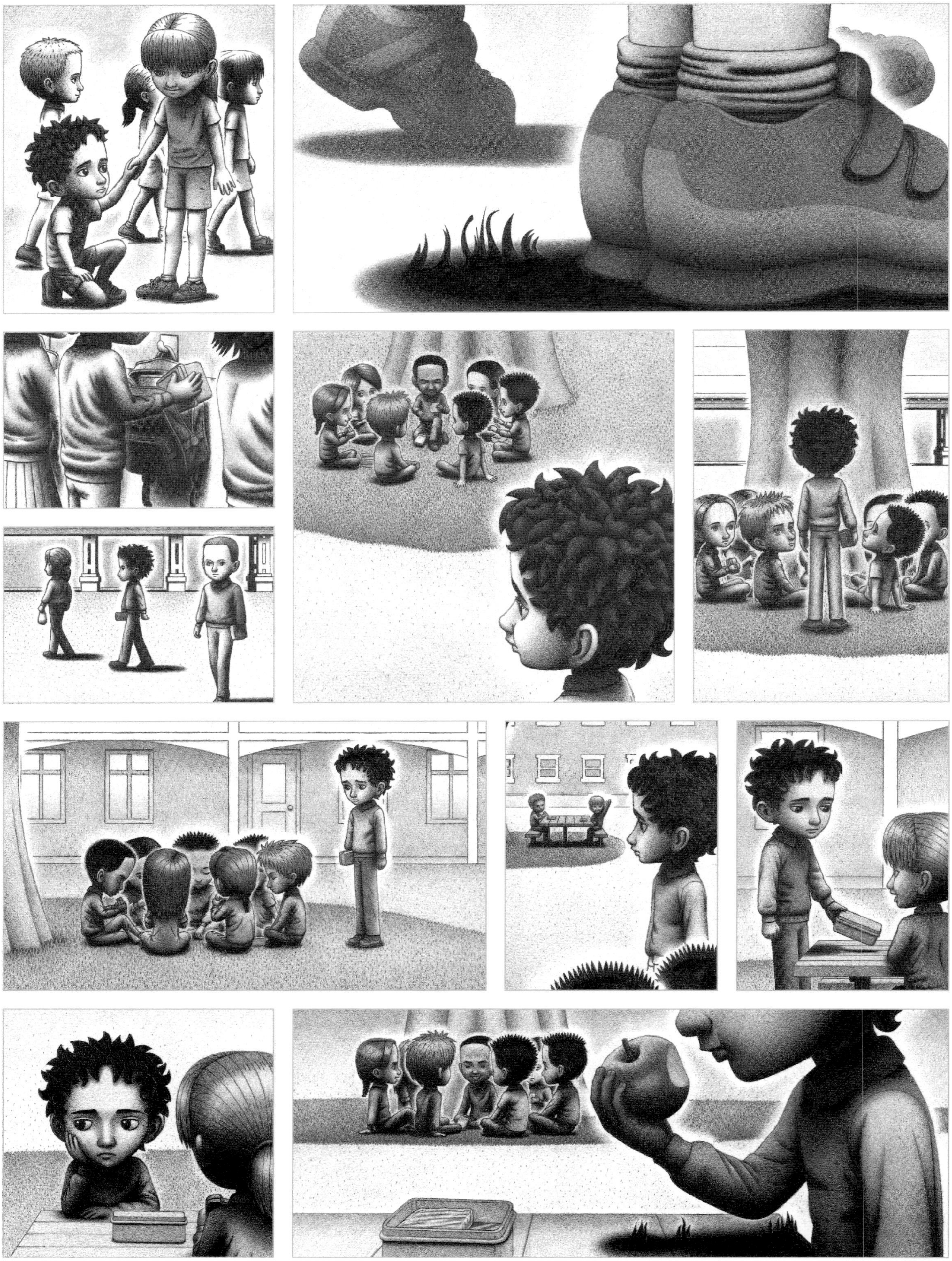

er sees an octopt
topuses come al
e diver counts a t
How many
ld there be?

_____

_____

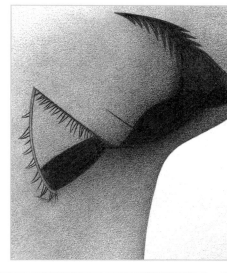

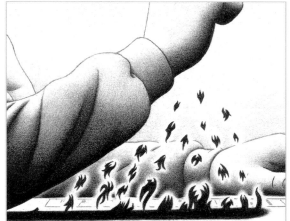

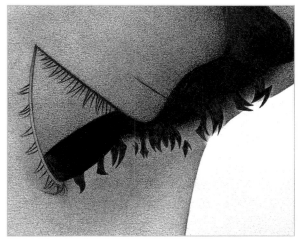

octopuses co
he diver counts
es. How many
ould there be?

_____

_____

jellyfish in one group
sh in another group.
me along and eat 34
How many jellyfish

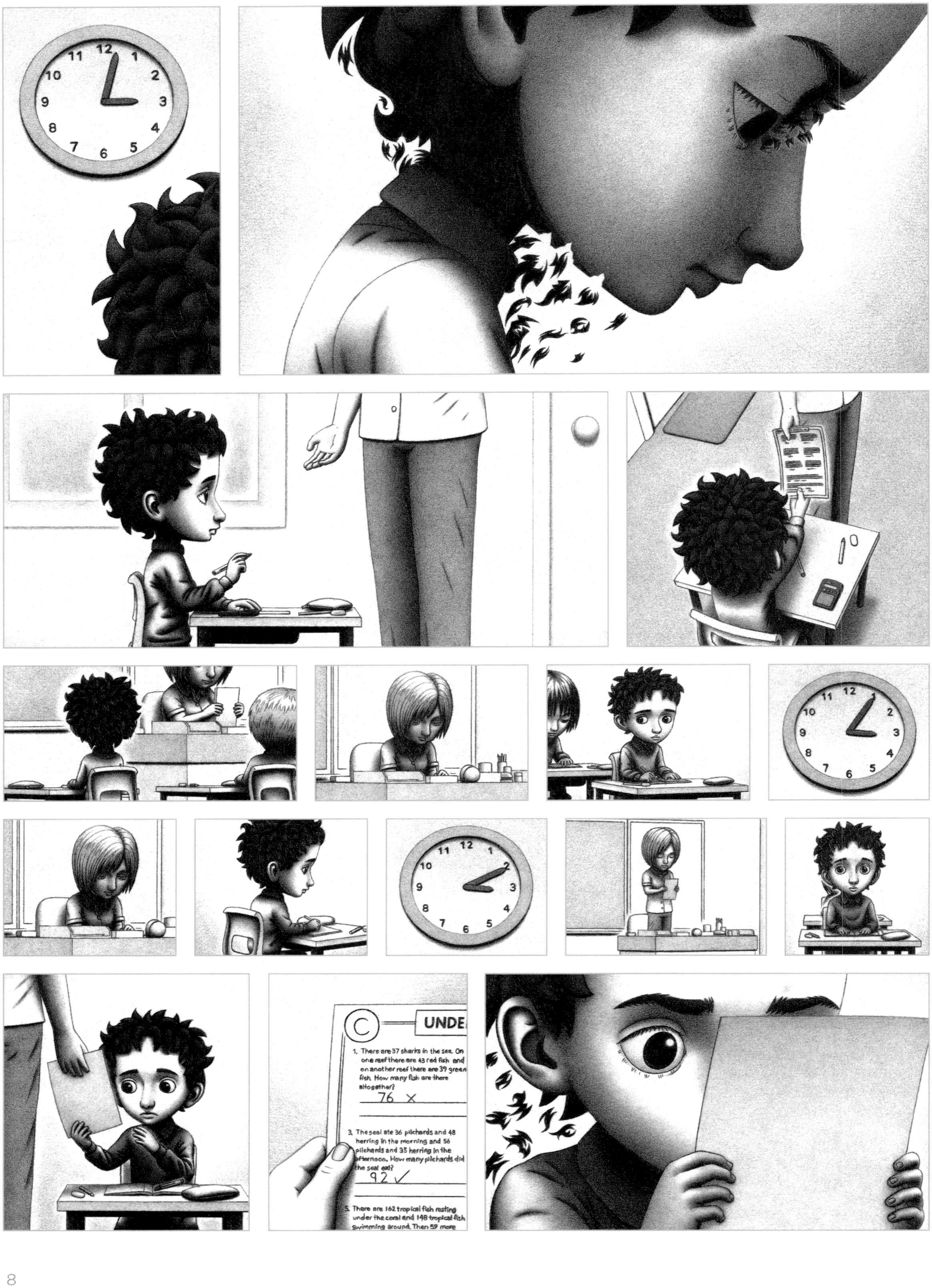
C
UNDE
1. There are 37 sharks in the sea. On one reef there are 43 red fish and on another reef there are 39 green fish. How many fish are there altogether?
76 ✗
3. The seal ate 36 pilchards and 48 herring in the morning and 56 pilchards and 35 herring in the afternoon. How many pilchards did the seal eat?
92 ✓
5. There are 162 tropical fish resting under the coral and 148 tropical fish swimming around. Then 59 more

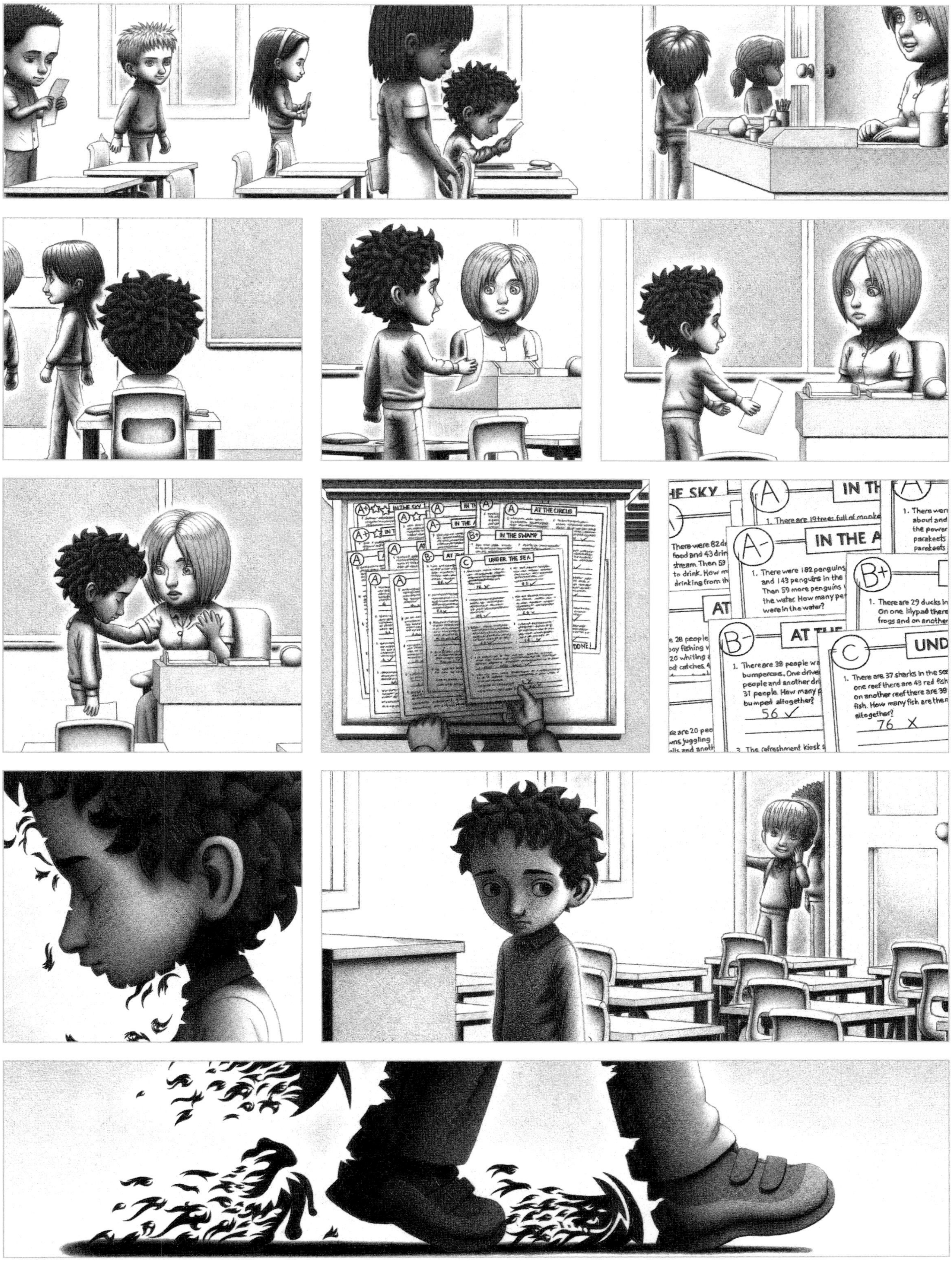

IN THE SKY
AT THE CIRCUS
IN THE SWAMP
UNDER THE SEA
DONE!
A
1. There are 19 trees full of monke
A-
IN THE A
1. There were 182 penguins
and 143 penguins in the
Then 59 more penguins
the water. How many pe
were in the water?
B+
1. There are 29 ducks in
On one lilypad there
frogs and on another
B-
AT THE
1. There are 38 people w
bumpercars. One driver
people and another dr
31 people. How many p
bumped altogether?
56 ✓
3. The refreshment kiosk
C
UND
1. There are 37 sharks in the sea
one reef there are 43 red fish
on another reef there are 39
fish. How many fish are the
altogether?
76 X

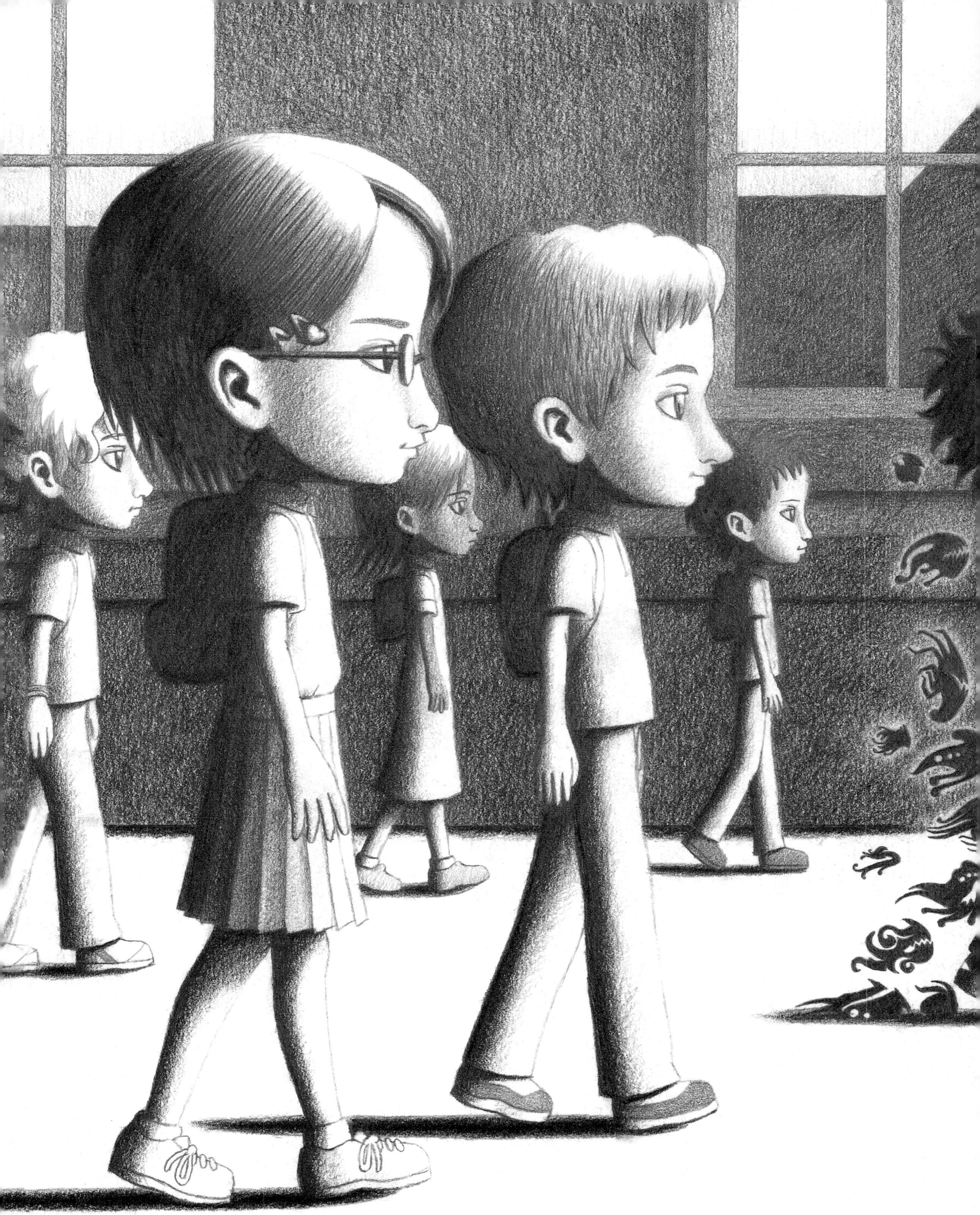

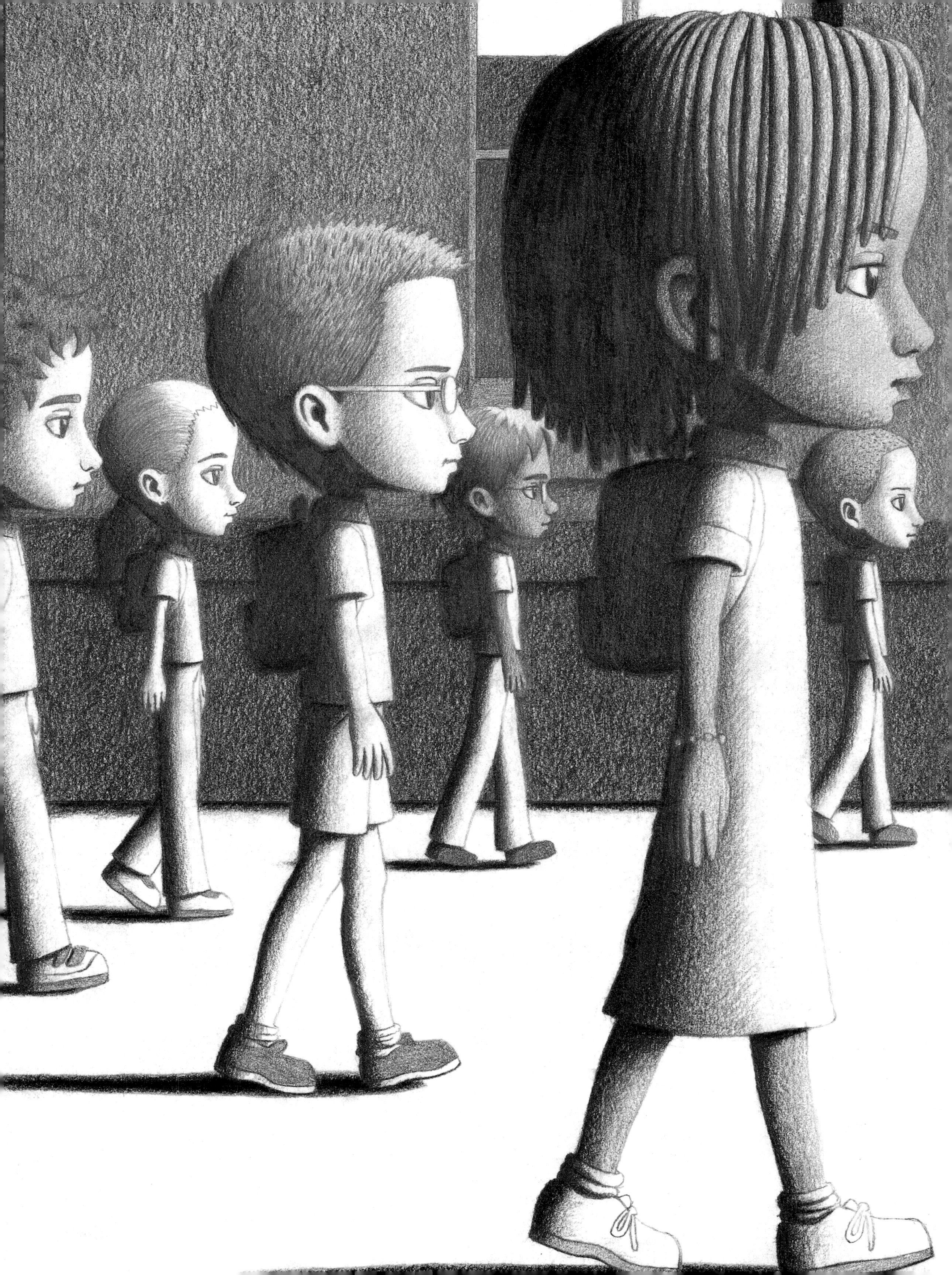

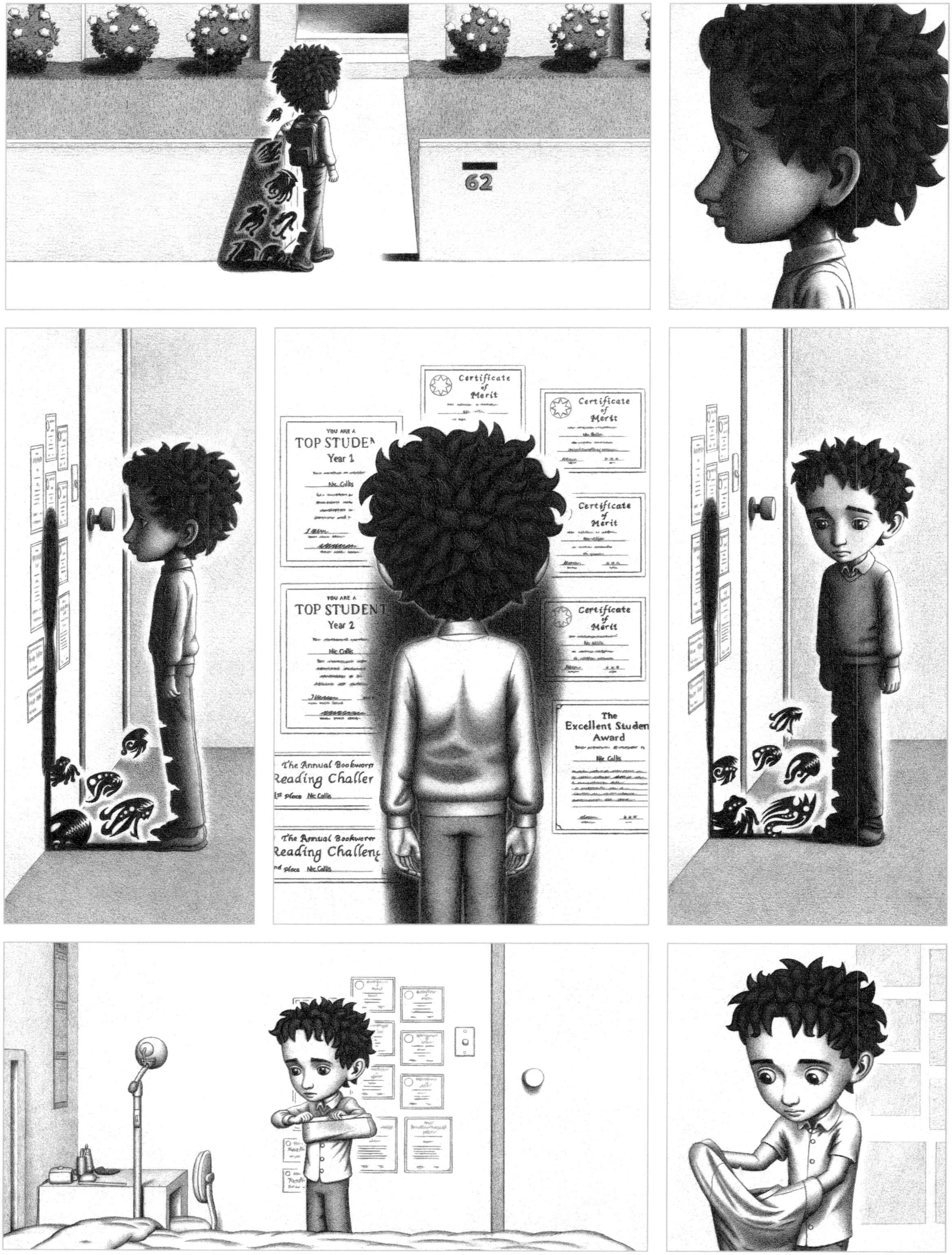
62
Certificate of Merit
YOU ARE A
TOP STUDEN
Year 1
Nic Collis
Certificate of Merit
Certificate of Merit
YOU ARE A
TOP STUDENT
Year 2
Nic Collis
Certificate of Merit
The Excellent Studen
Award
Nic Collis
The Annual Bookworm
Reading Challer
1st Place Nic Collis
The Annual Bookworm
Reading Challeng
2nd Place Nic Collis

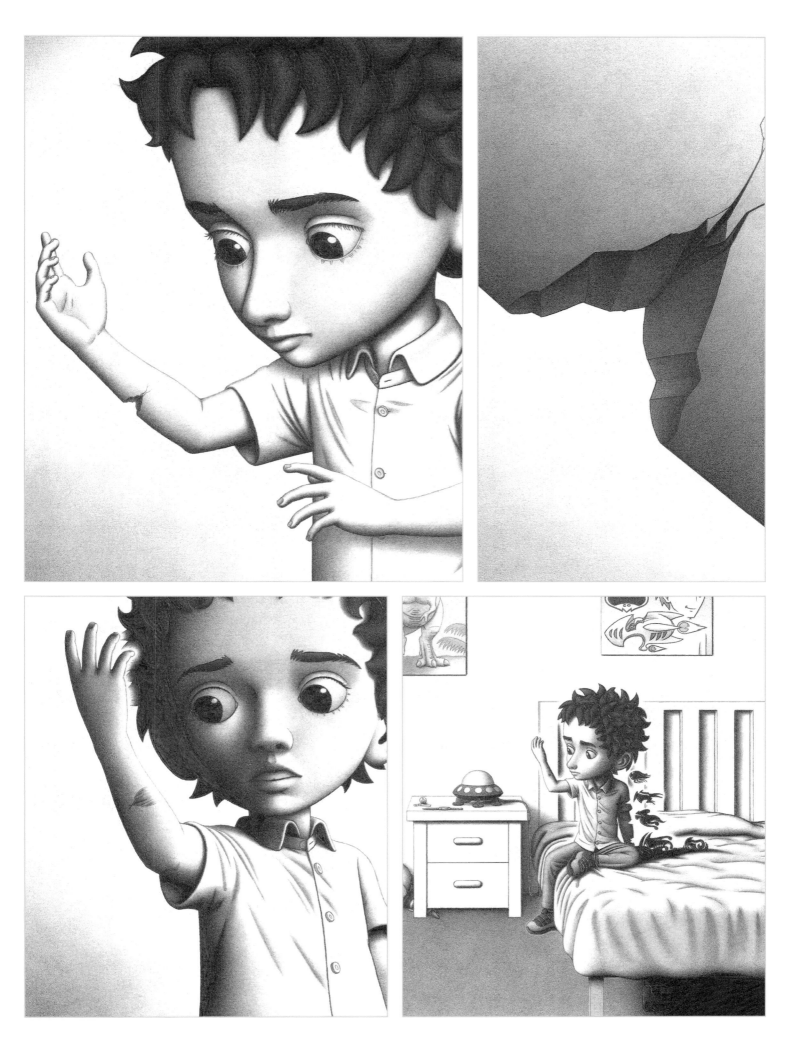

bag only holds 5 marbles
g holds 12 marbles. 99
ere bought when more
gs were sold. How many
e of bag were sold?

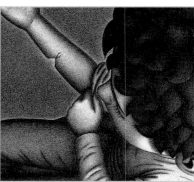

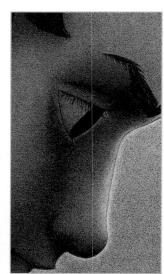

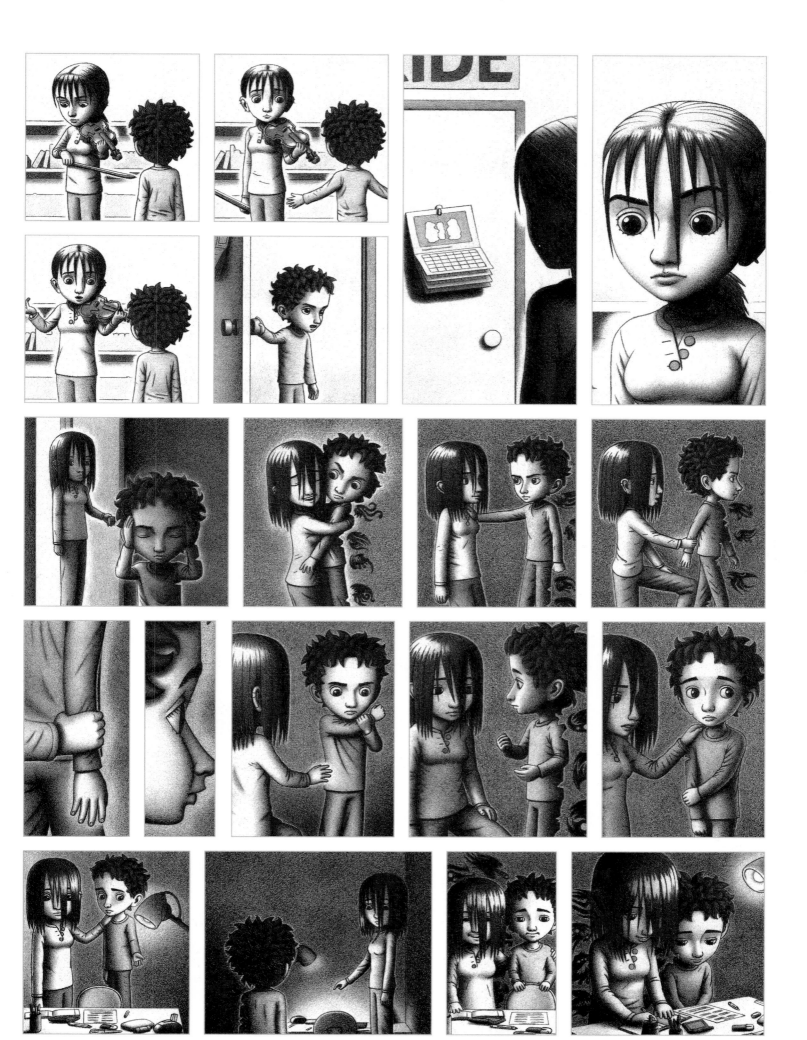

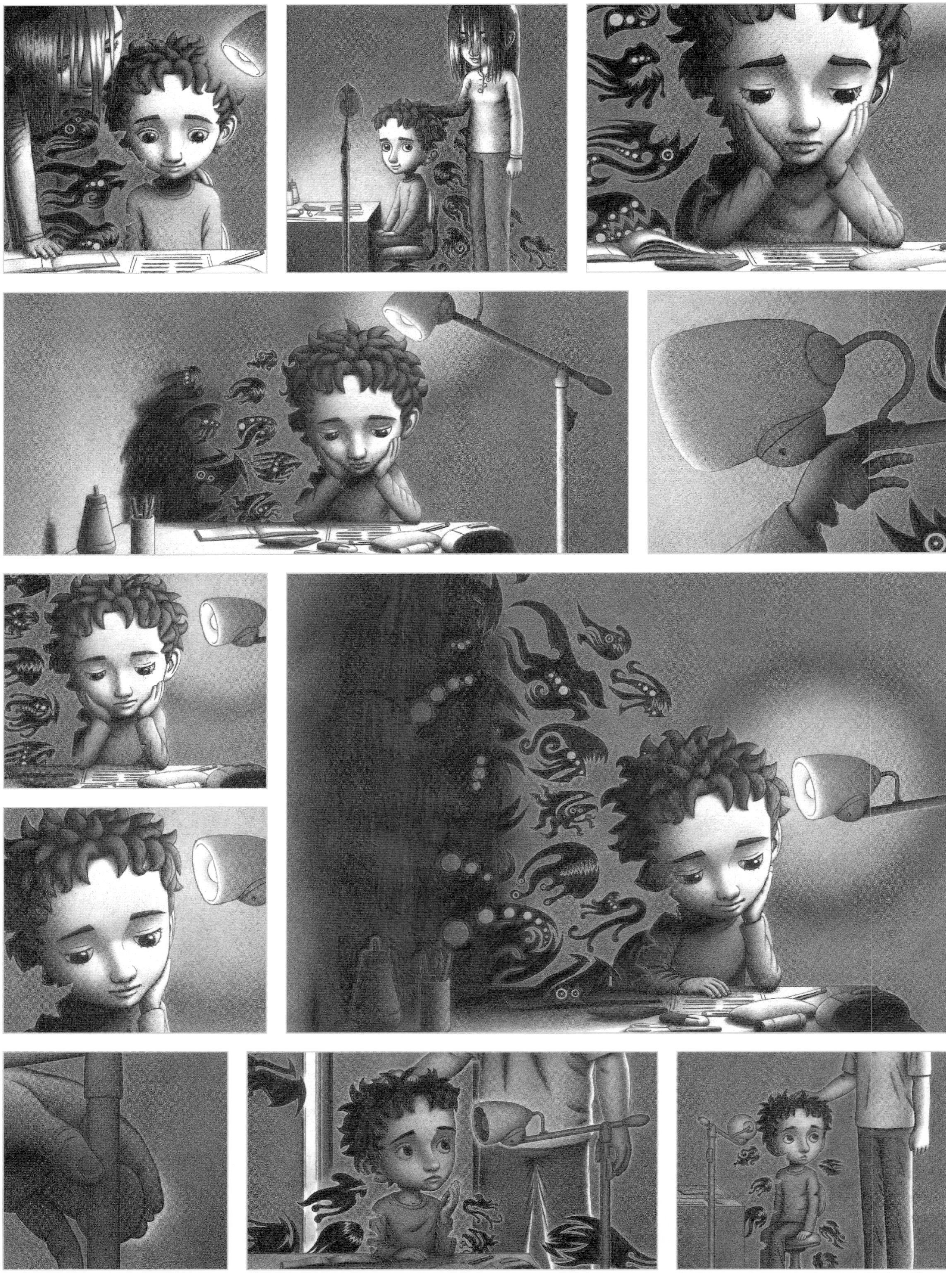

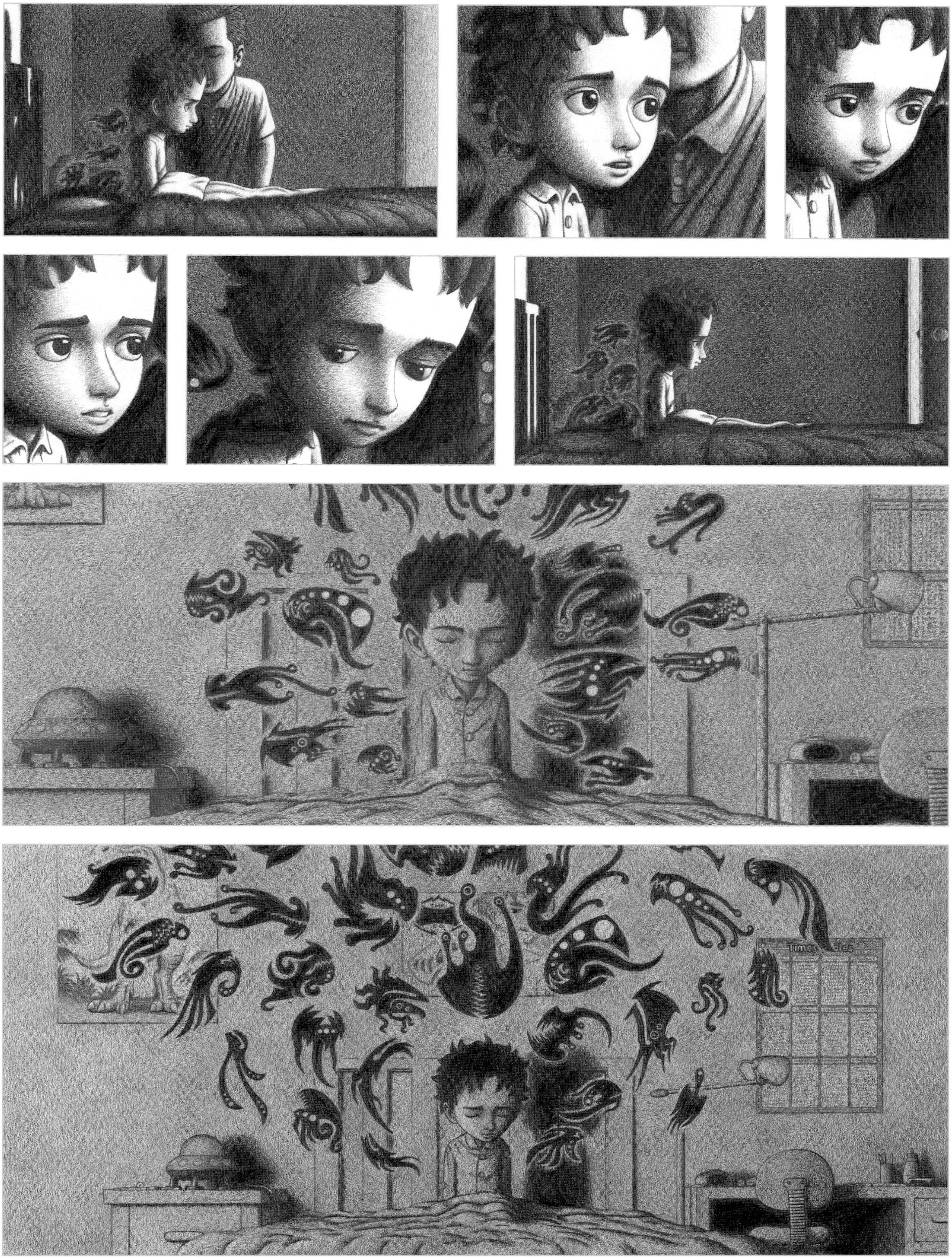
Times

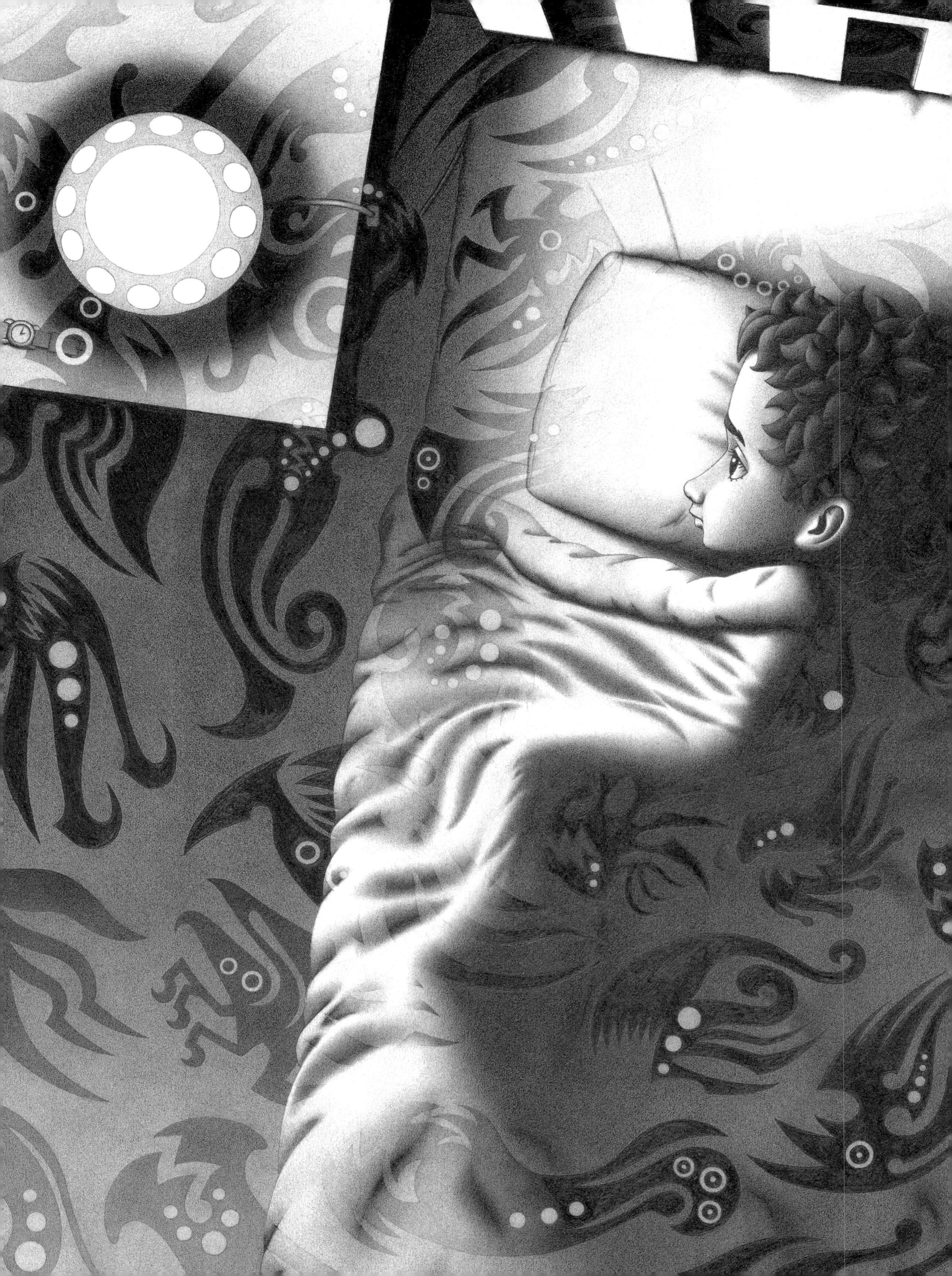

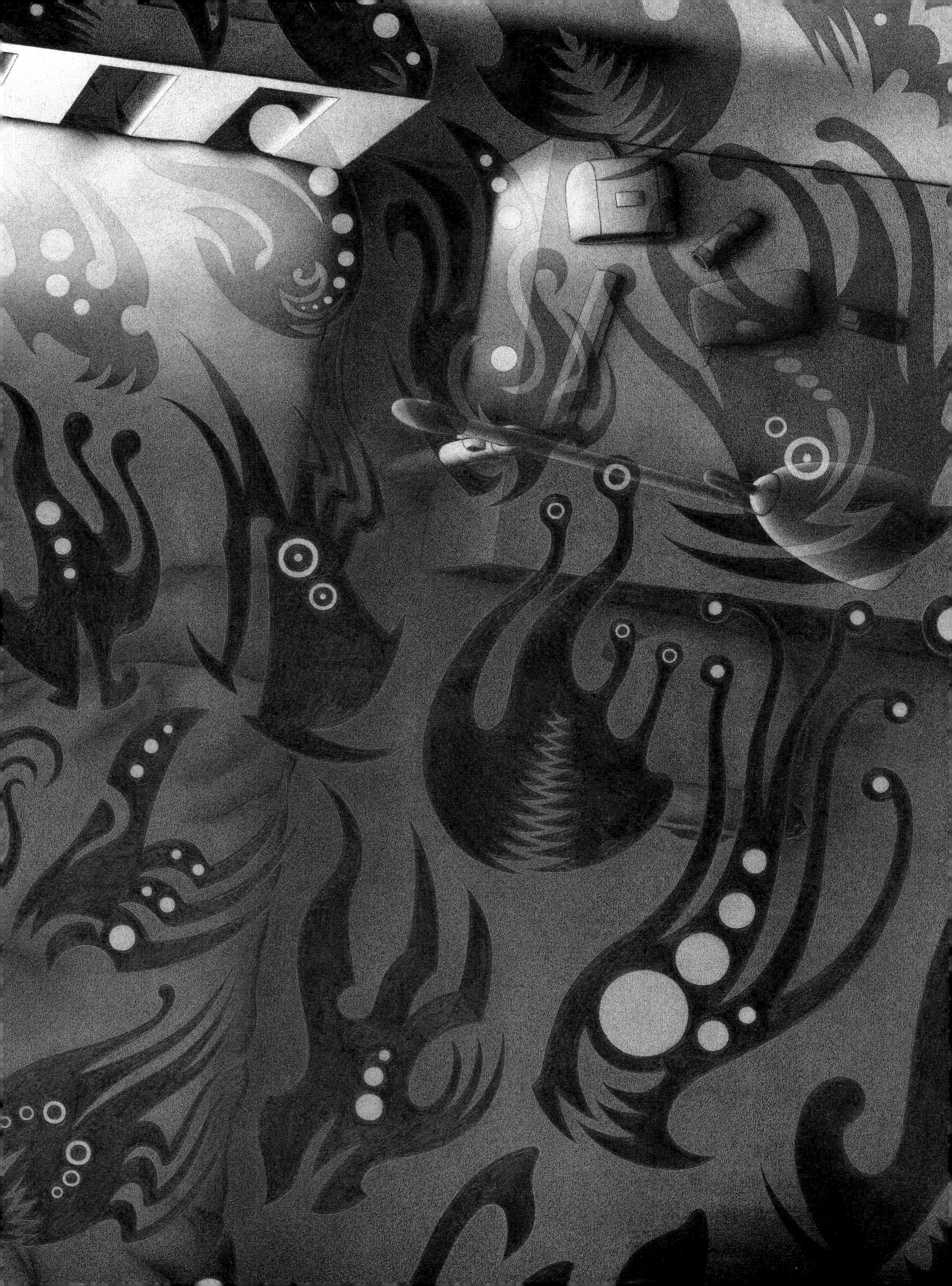

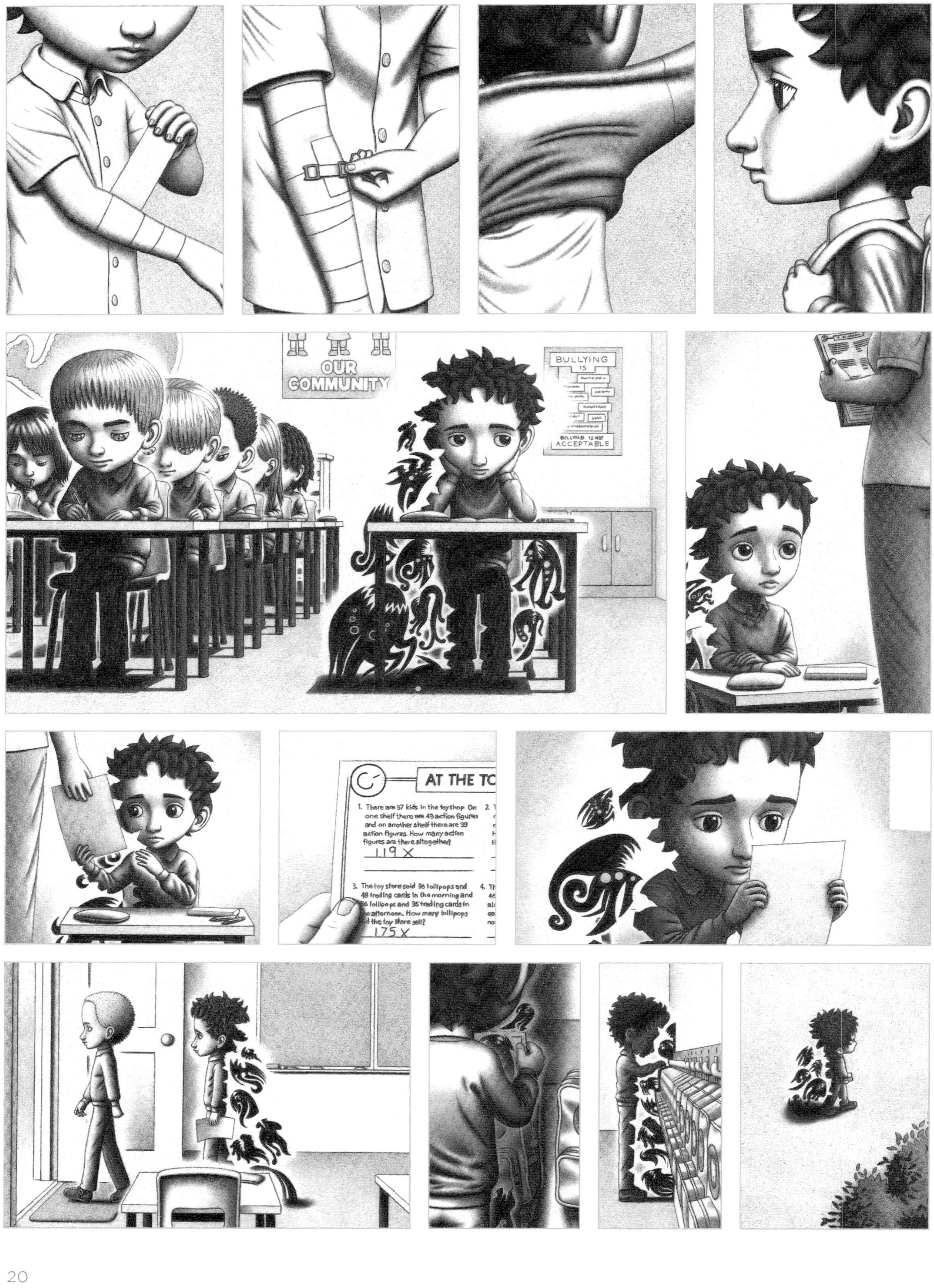
OUR COMMUNITY
BULLYING IS
BULLYING IS NOT ACCEPTABLE
AT THE
1. There are 37 kids in the toyshop. On one shelf there are 43 action figures and on another shelf there are 39 action figures. How many action figures are there altogether?
119 X
3. The toy store sold 36 lollipops and 48 trading cards in the morning and
lollipops and 35 trading cards in
afternoon. How many lollipops
the toy store sell?
175 X

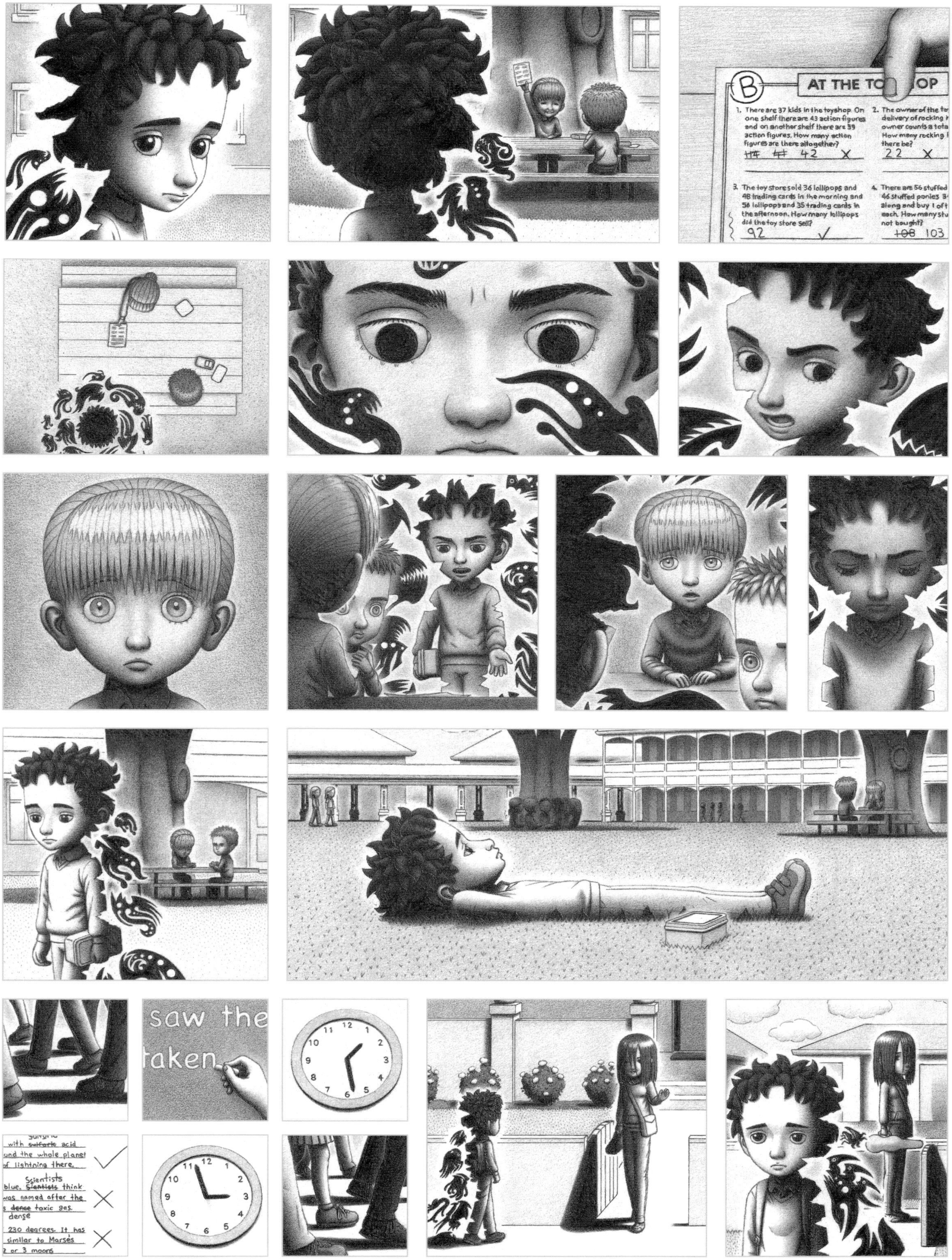

B
AT THE TO OP
1. There are 37 kids in the toyshop. On one shelf there are 43 action figures and on another shelf there are 39 action figures. How many action figures are there altogether?
42 X
2. The owner of the to
delivery of rocking
owner counts a tota
How many rocking
there be?
22 X
3. The toy store sold 36 lollipops and 48 trading cards in the morning and 56 lollipops and 35 trading cards in the afternoon. How many lollipops did the toy store sell?
92 ✓
4. There are 56 stuffed
46 stuffed ponies
along and buy 1 of t
each. How many stu
not bought?
103
saw the
taken
with acid
und the whole planet
of lightning there.
Scientists
blue. think
was named after the
toxic gas.
dense
230 degrees. It has
similar to Marses
2 or 3 moons

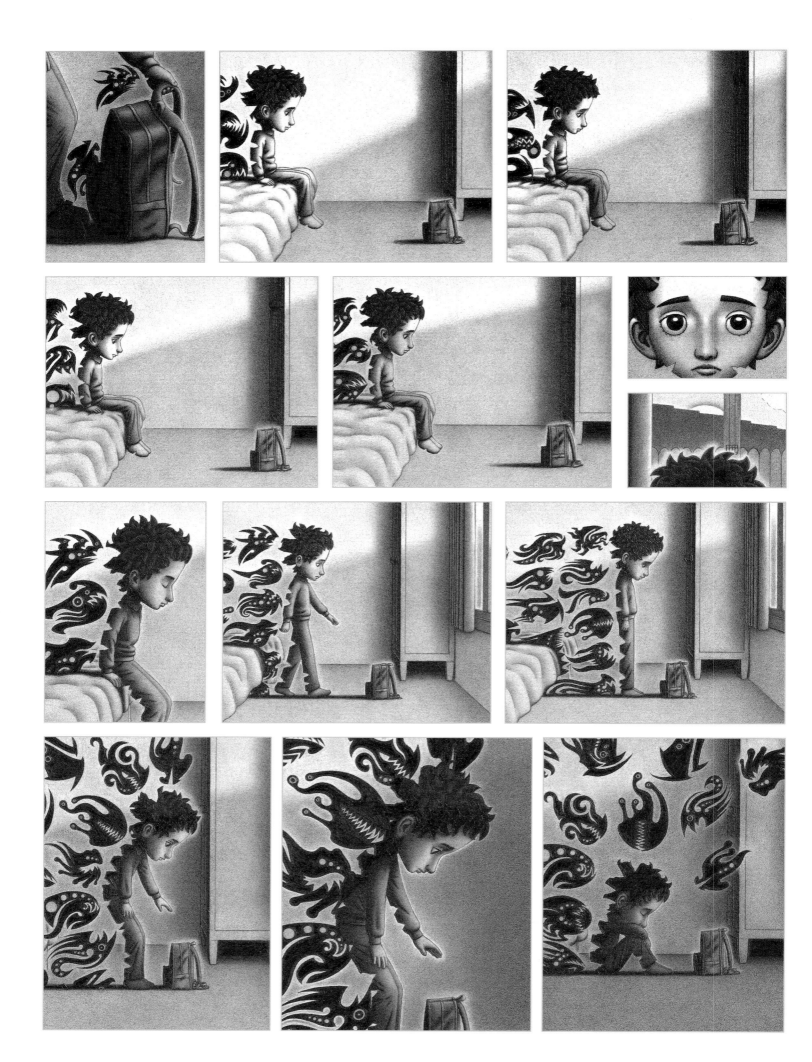

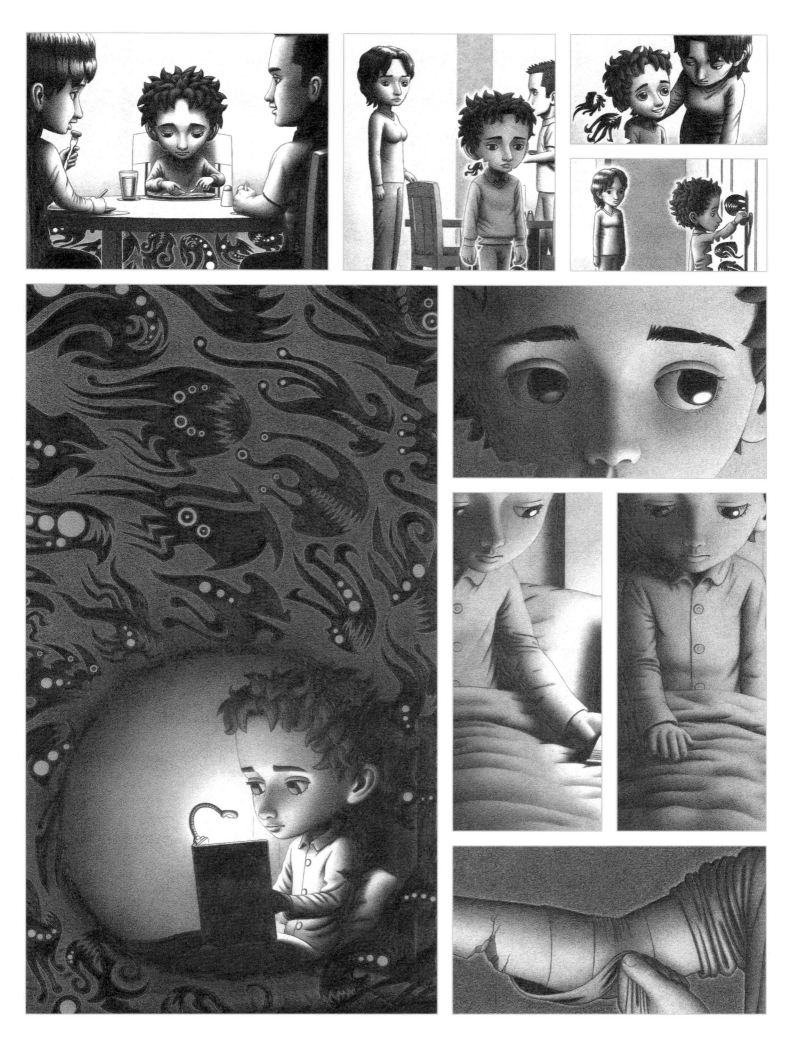

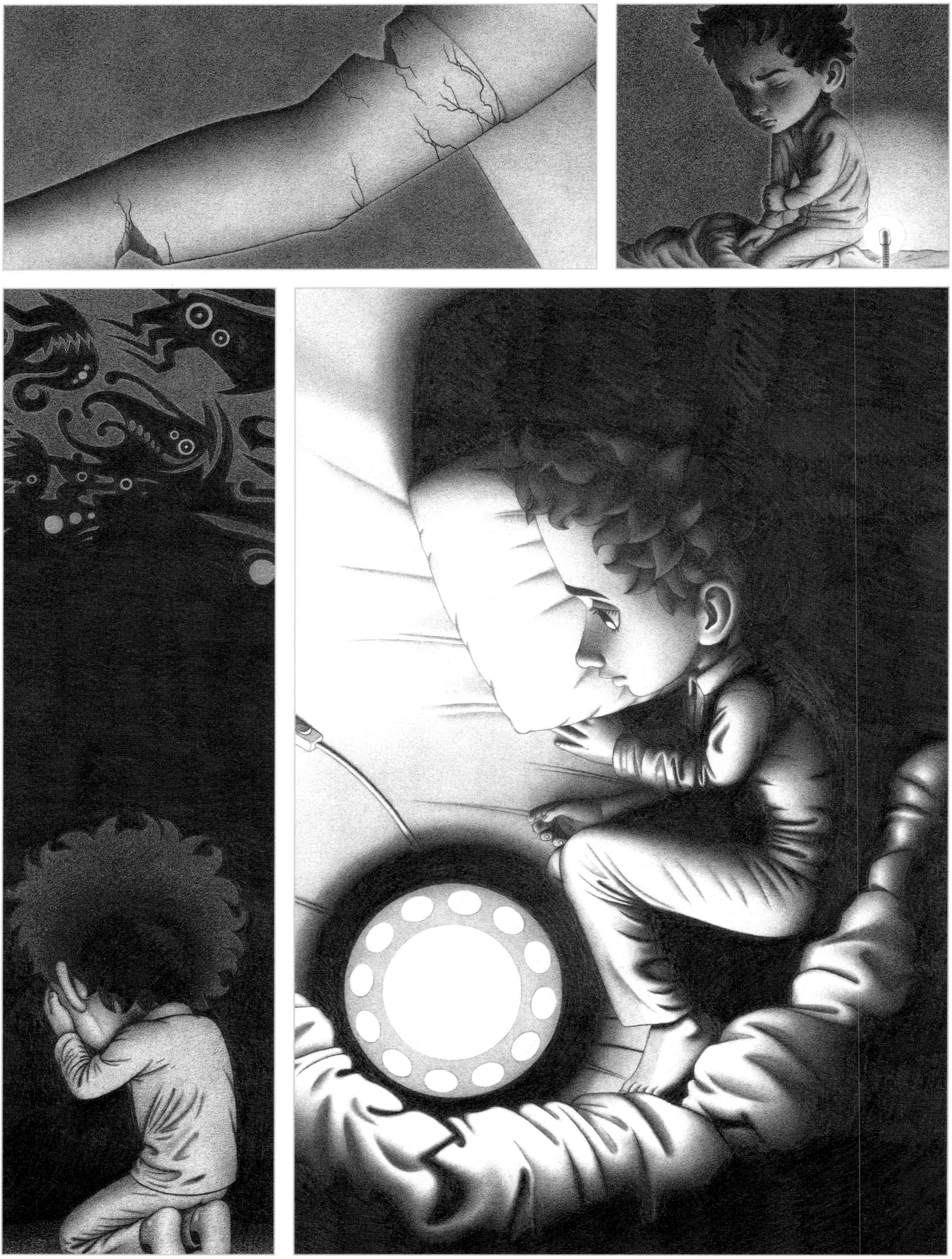

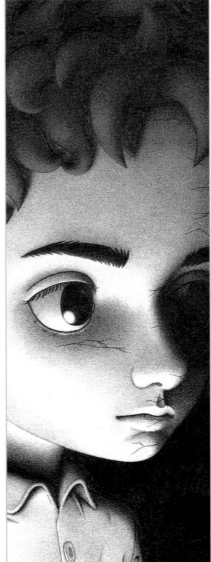

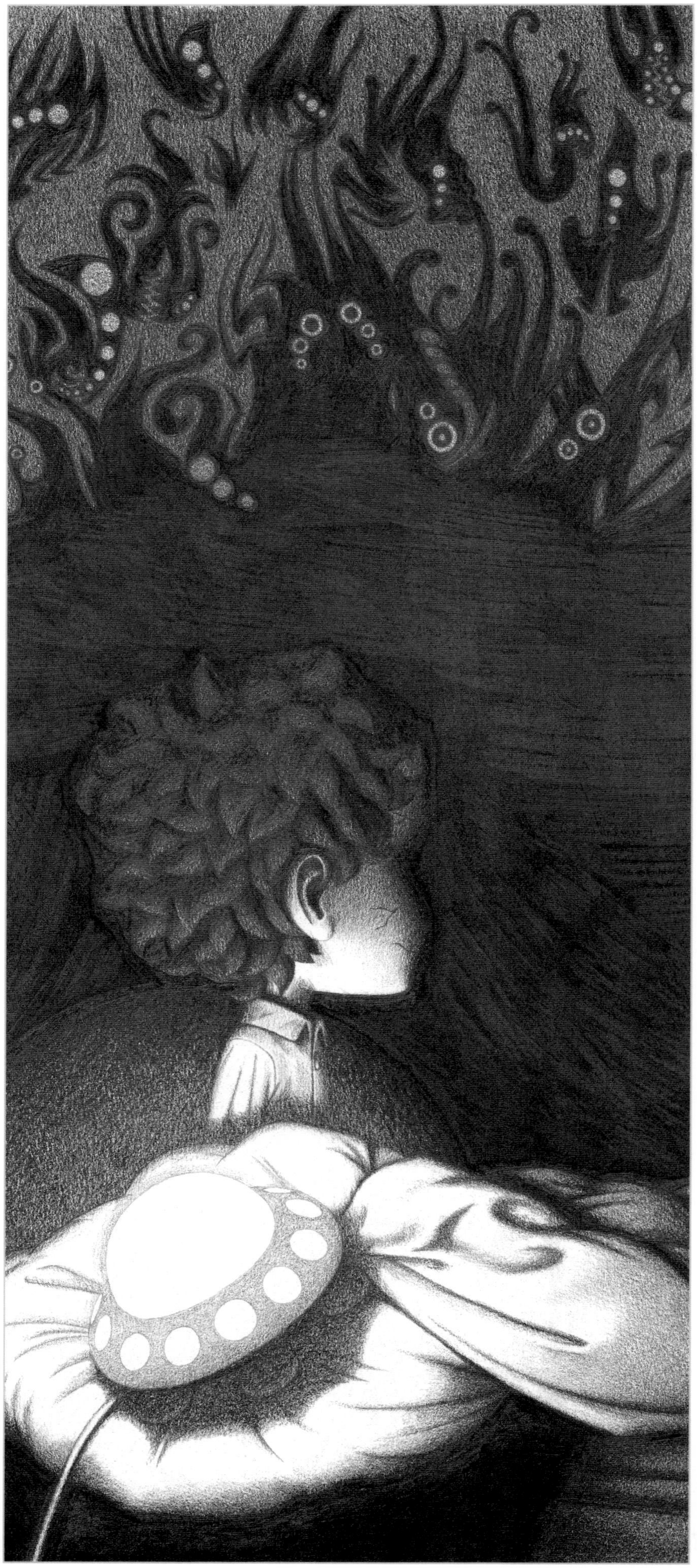

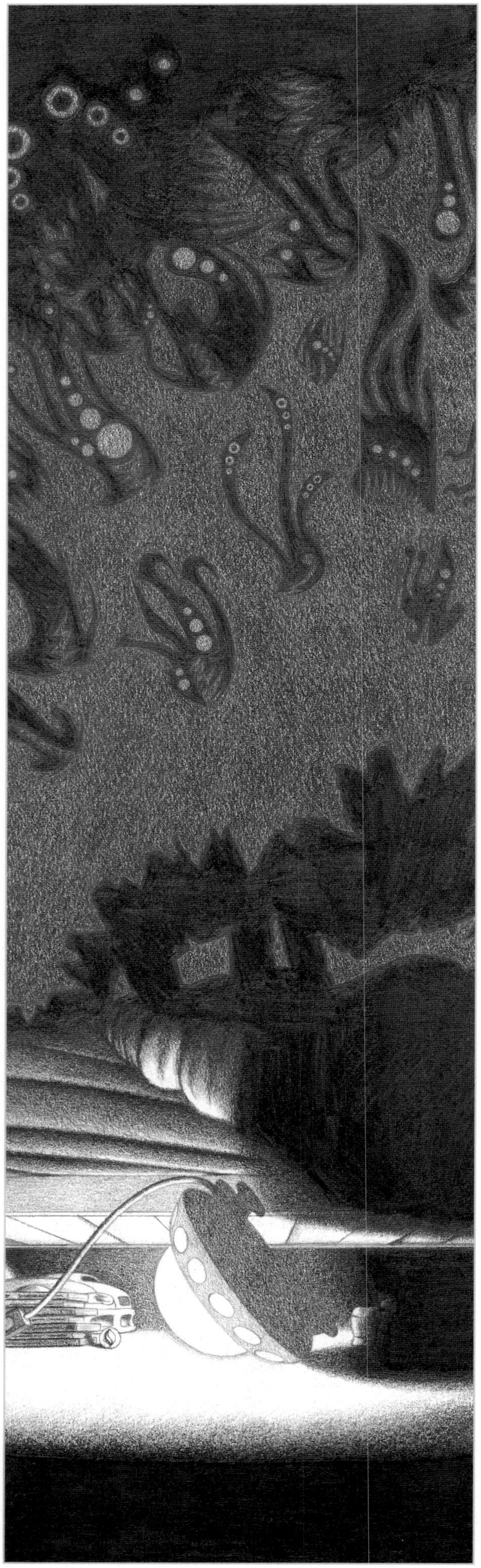

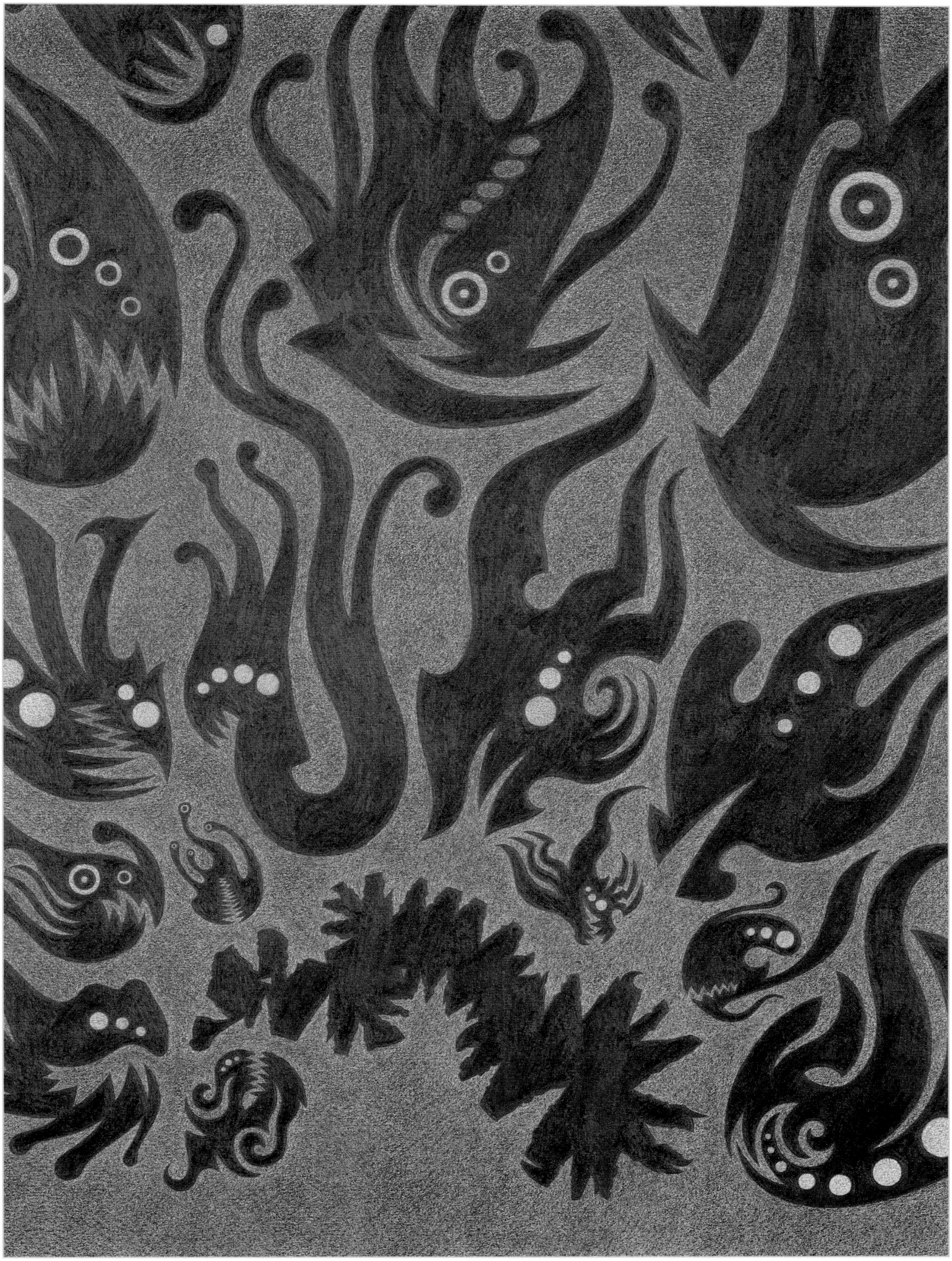

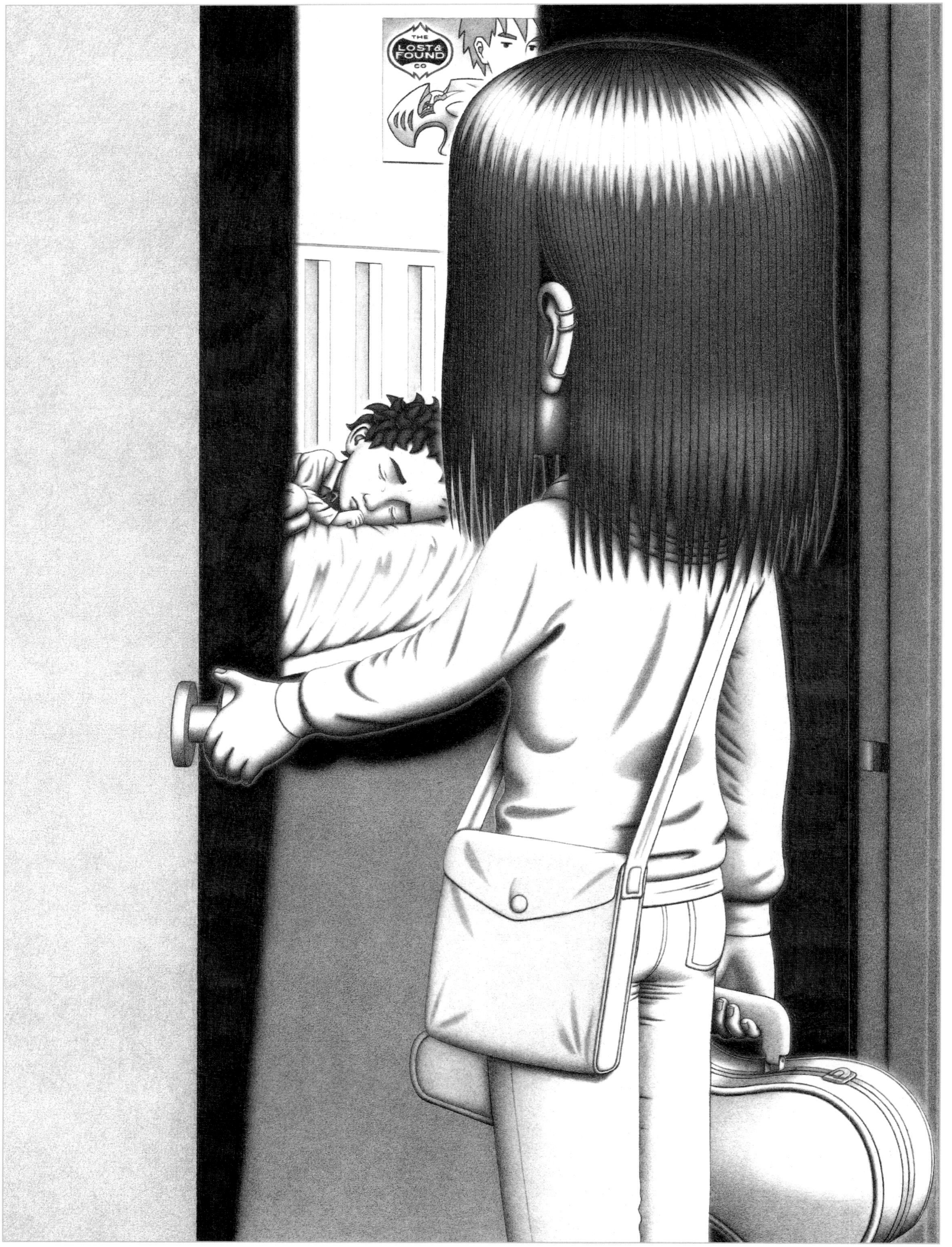
THE
LOST&
FOUND
CO

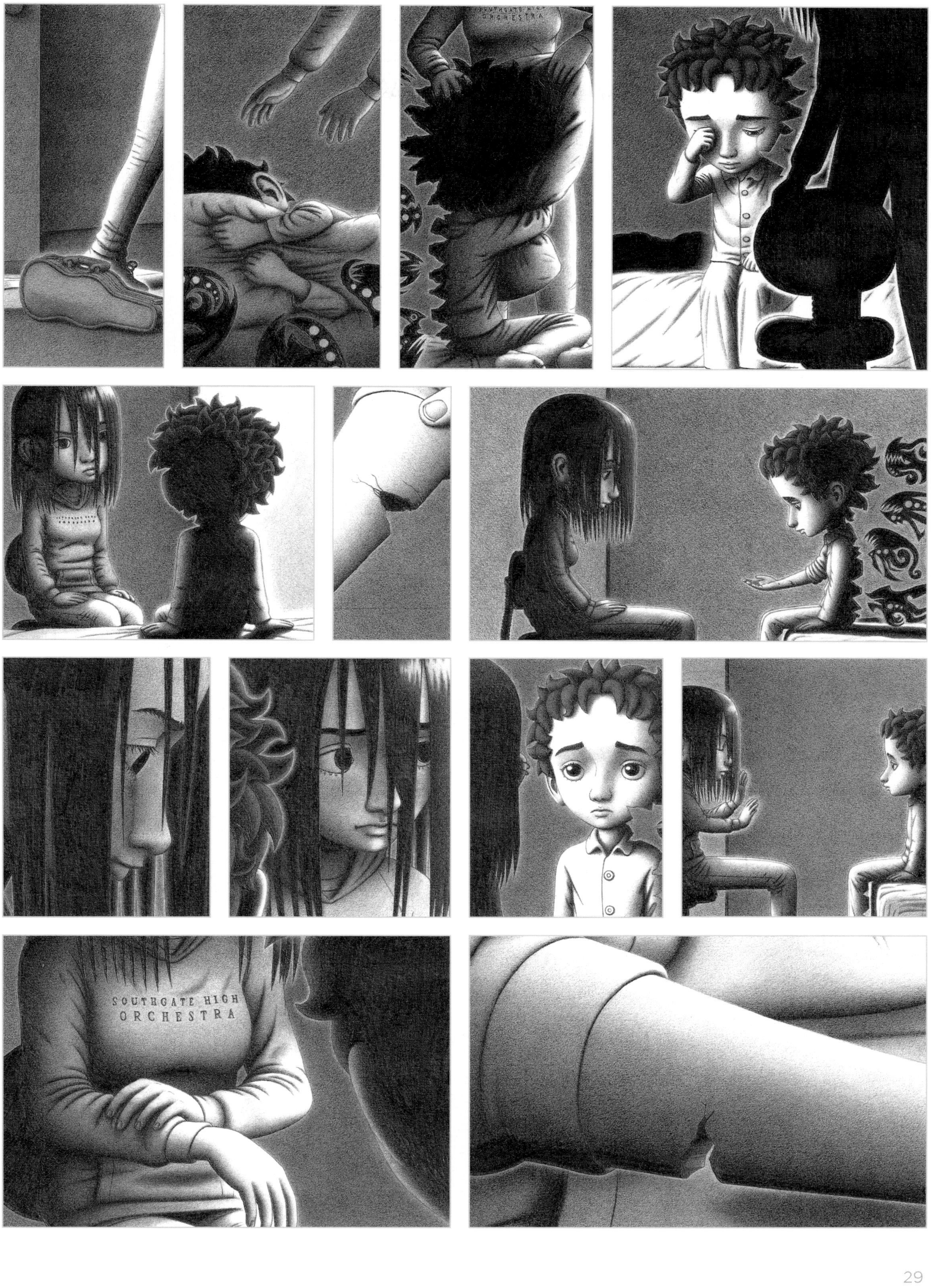
SOUTHGATE HIGH
ORCHESTRA

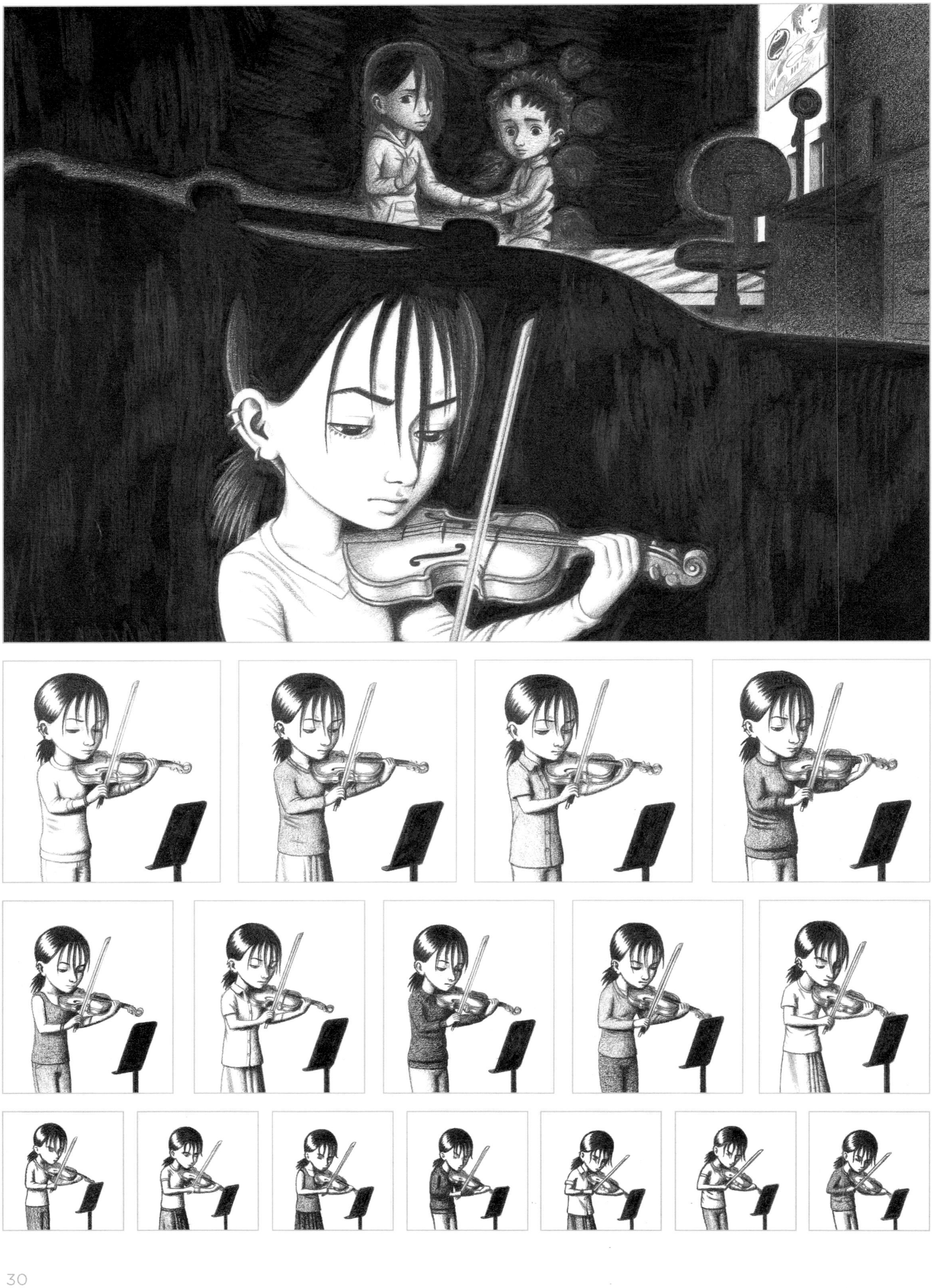

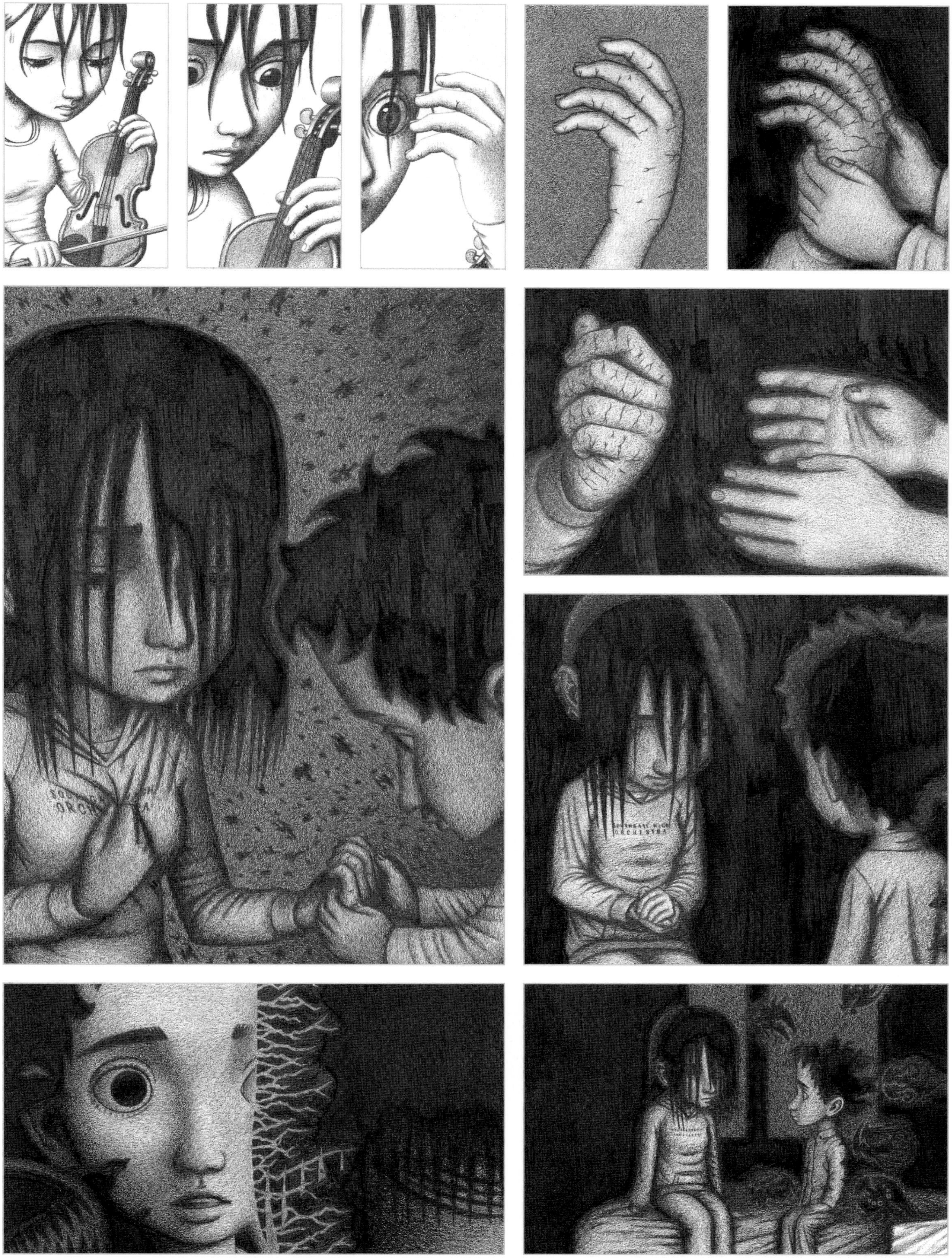
ORCHESTRA

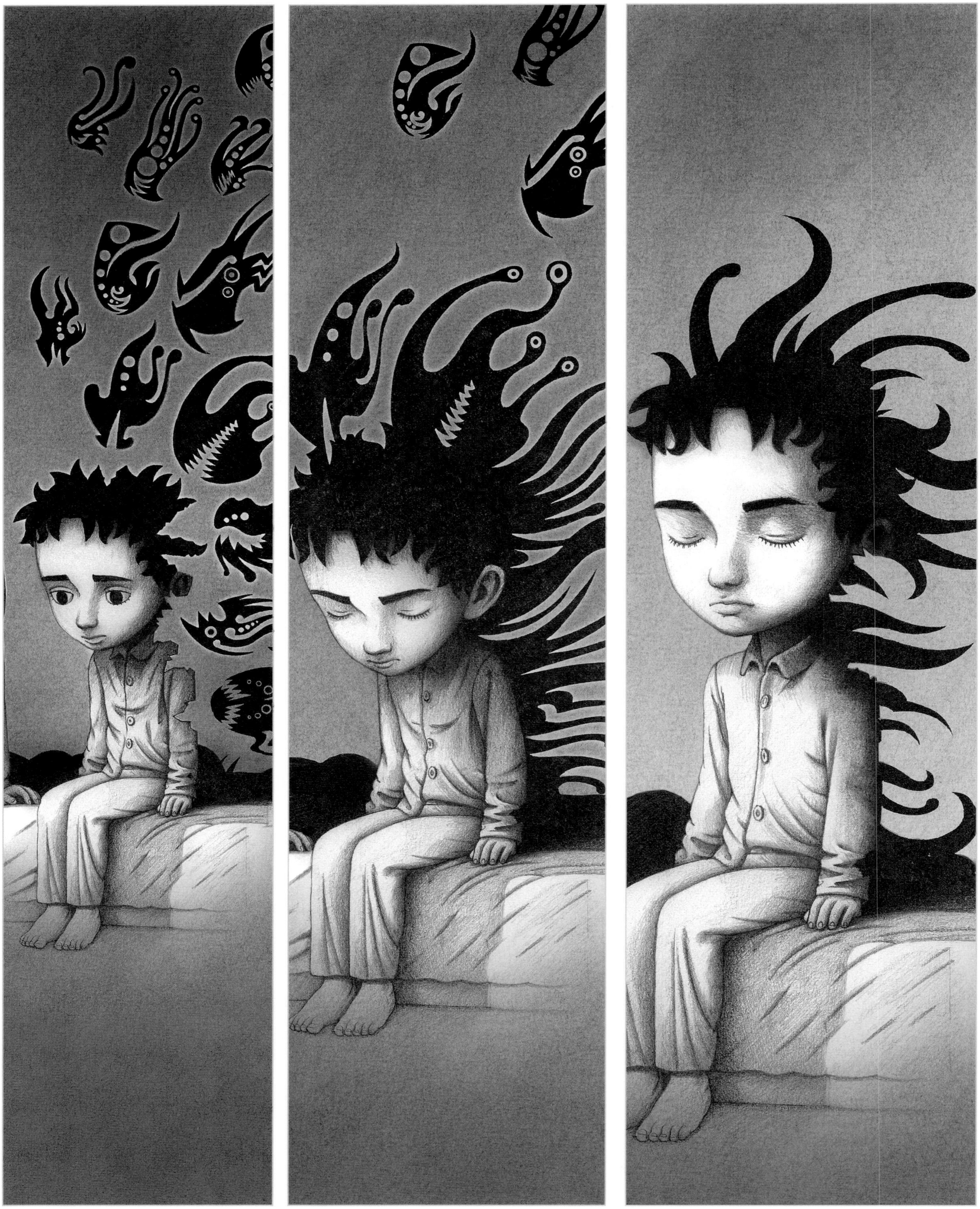

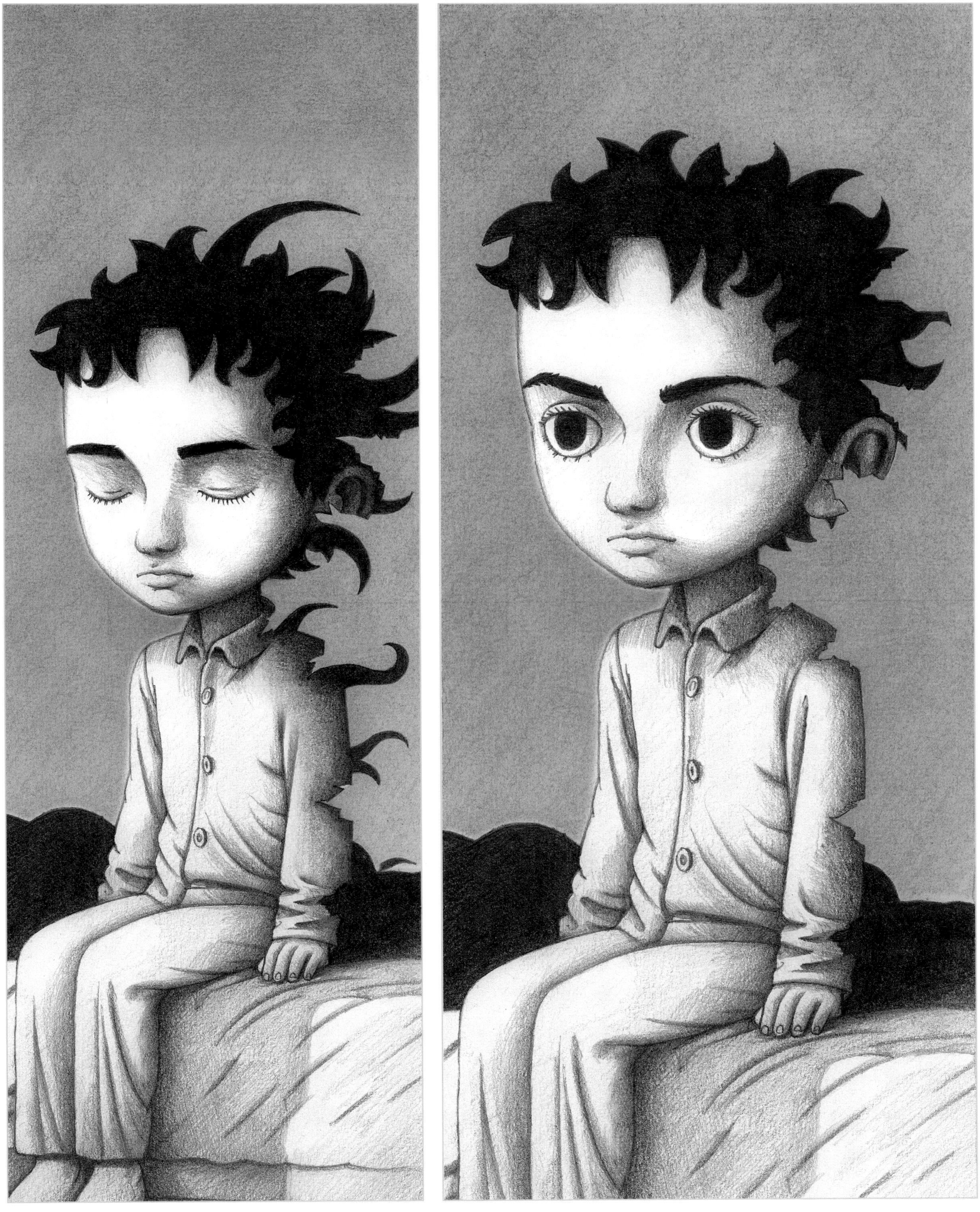

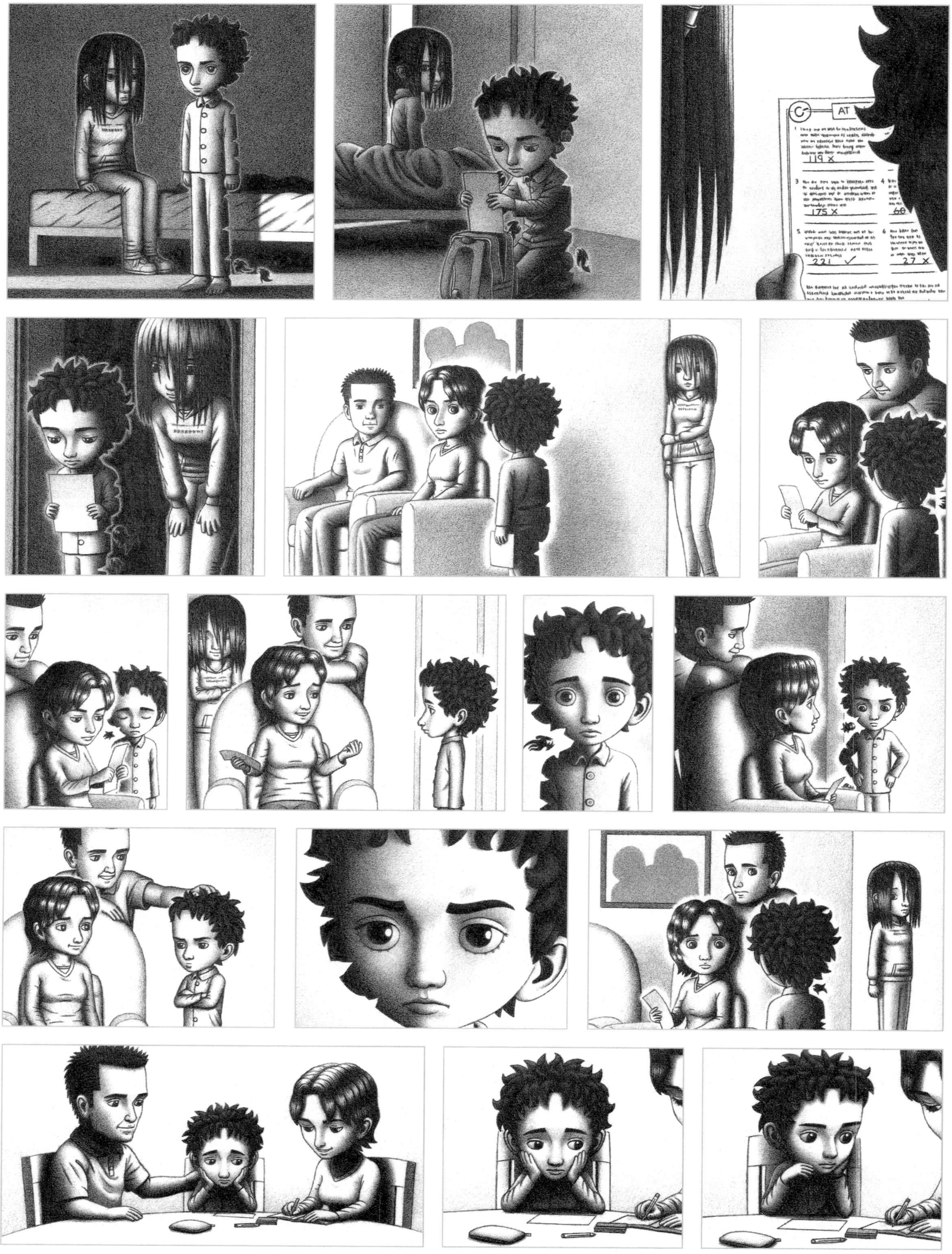
AT
119 X
175 X
221 ✓
27 X

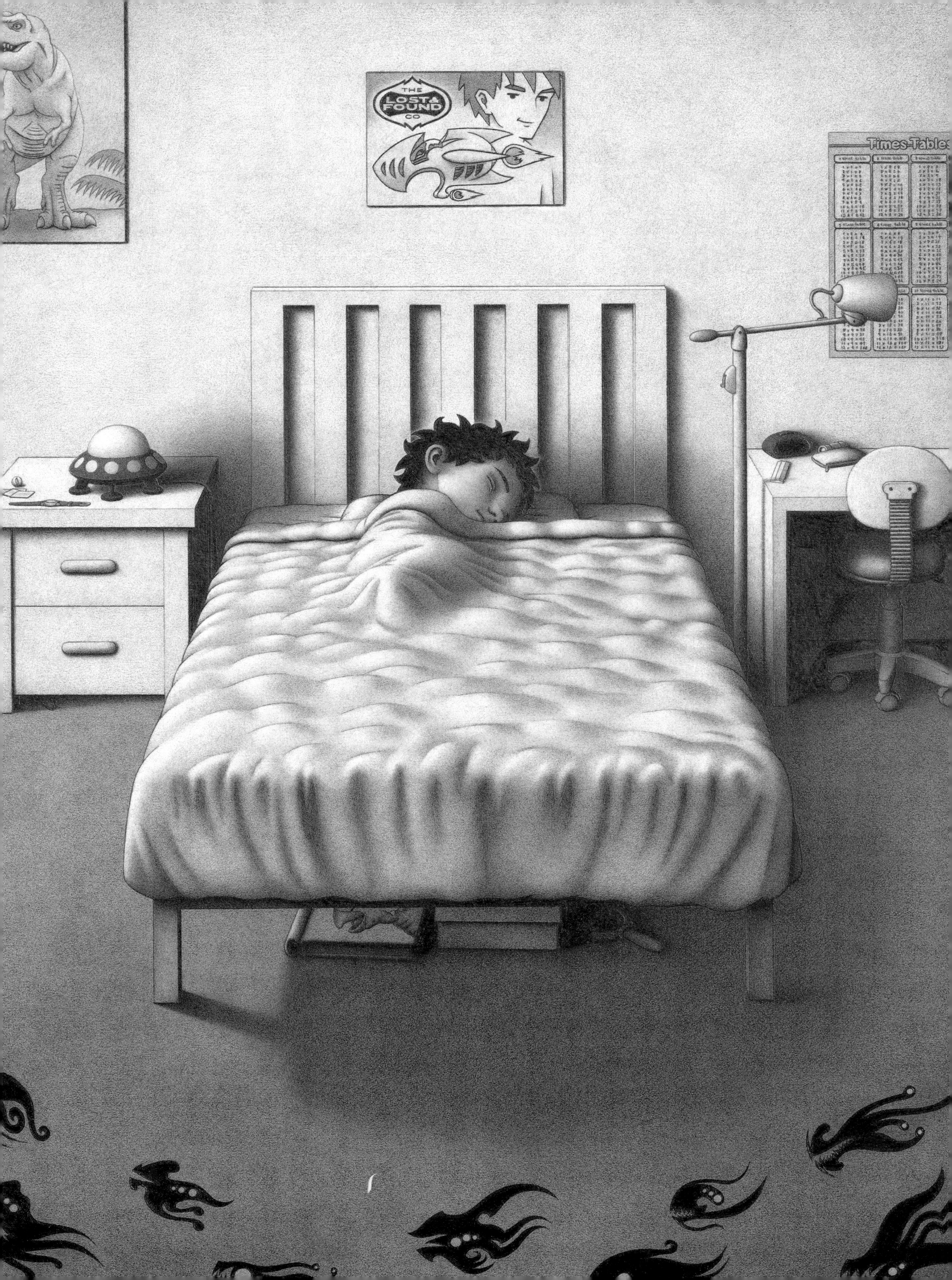
THE
LOST & FOUND
CO

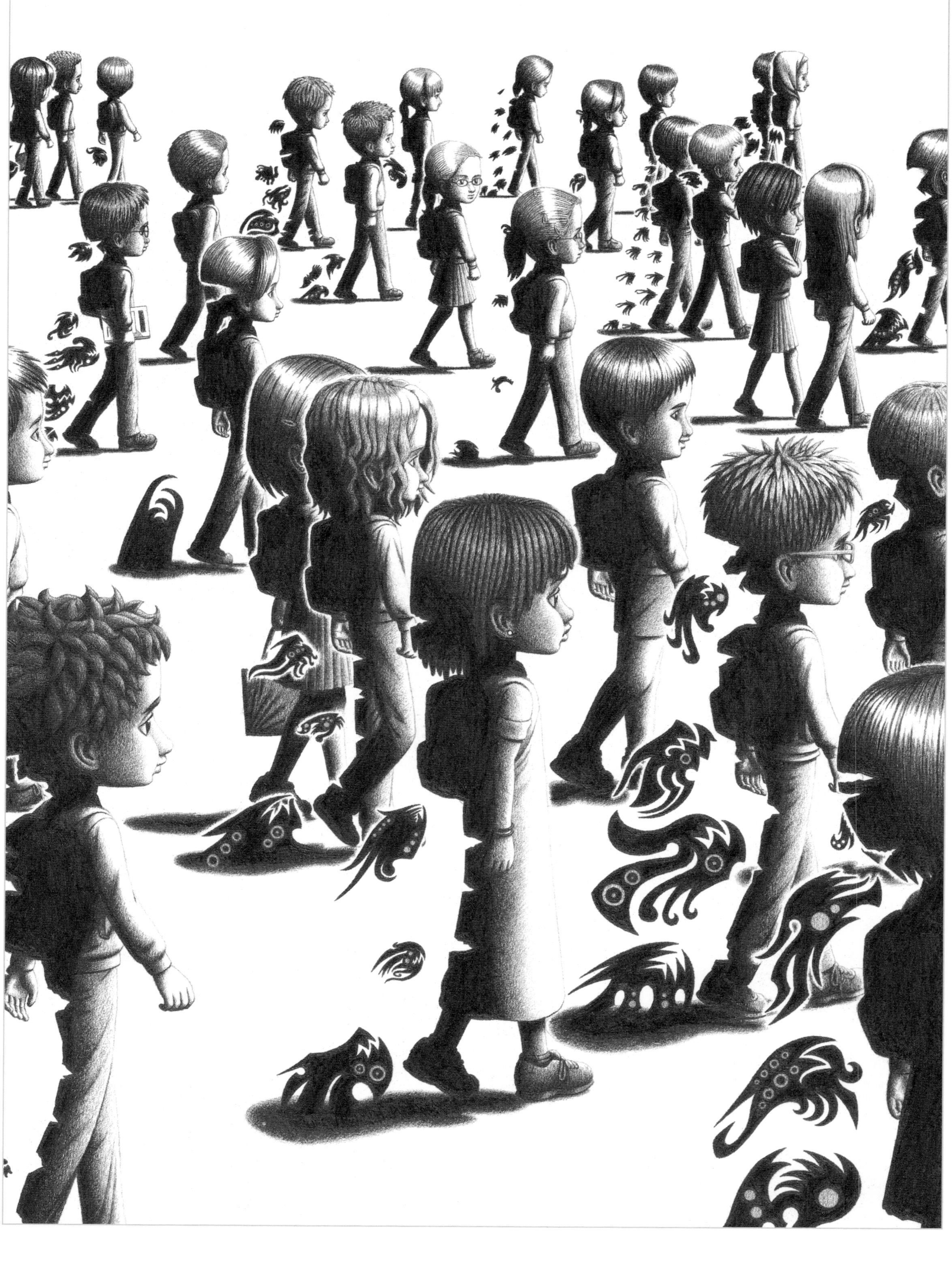

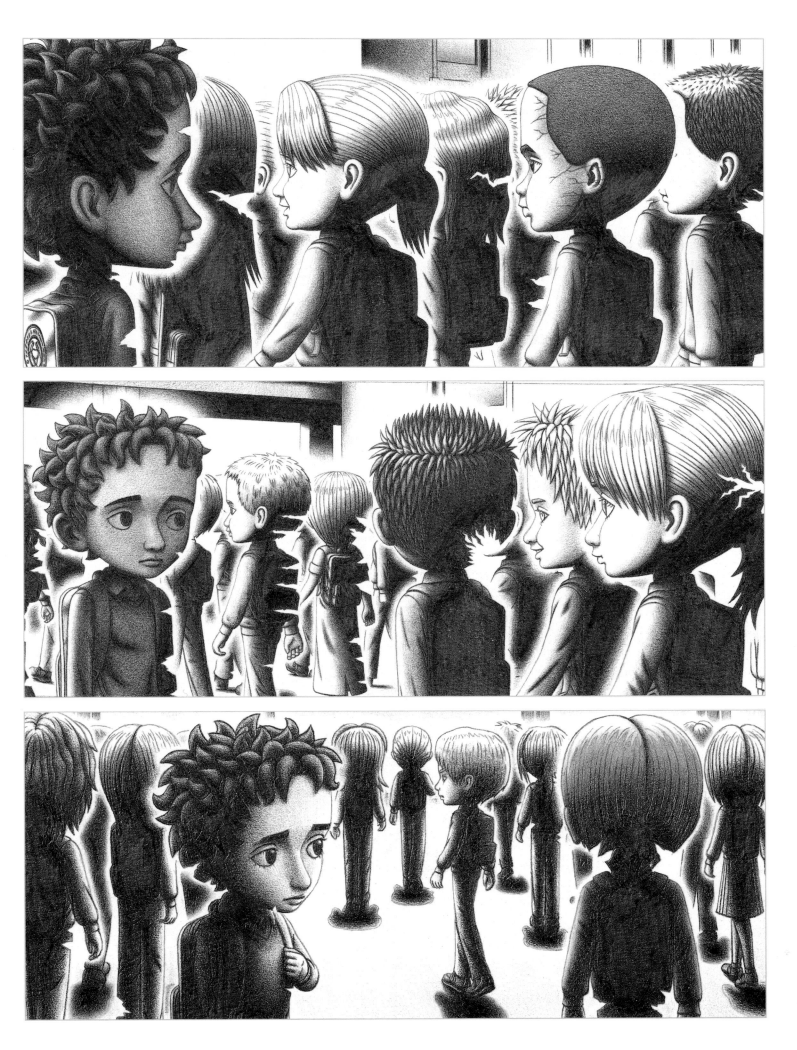

37

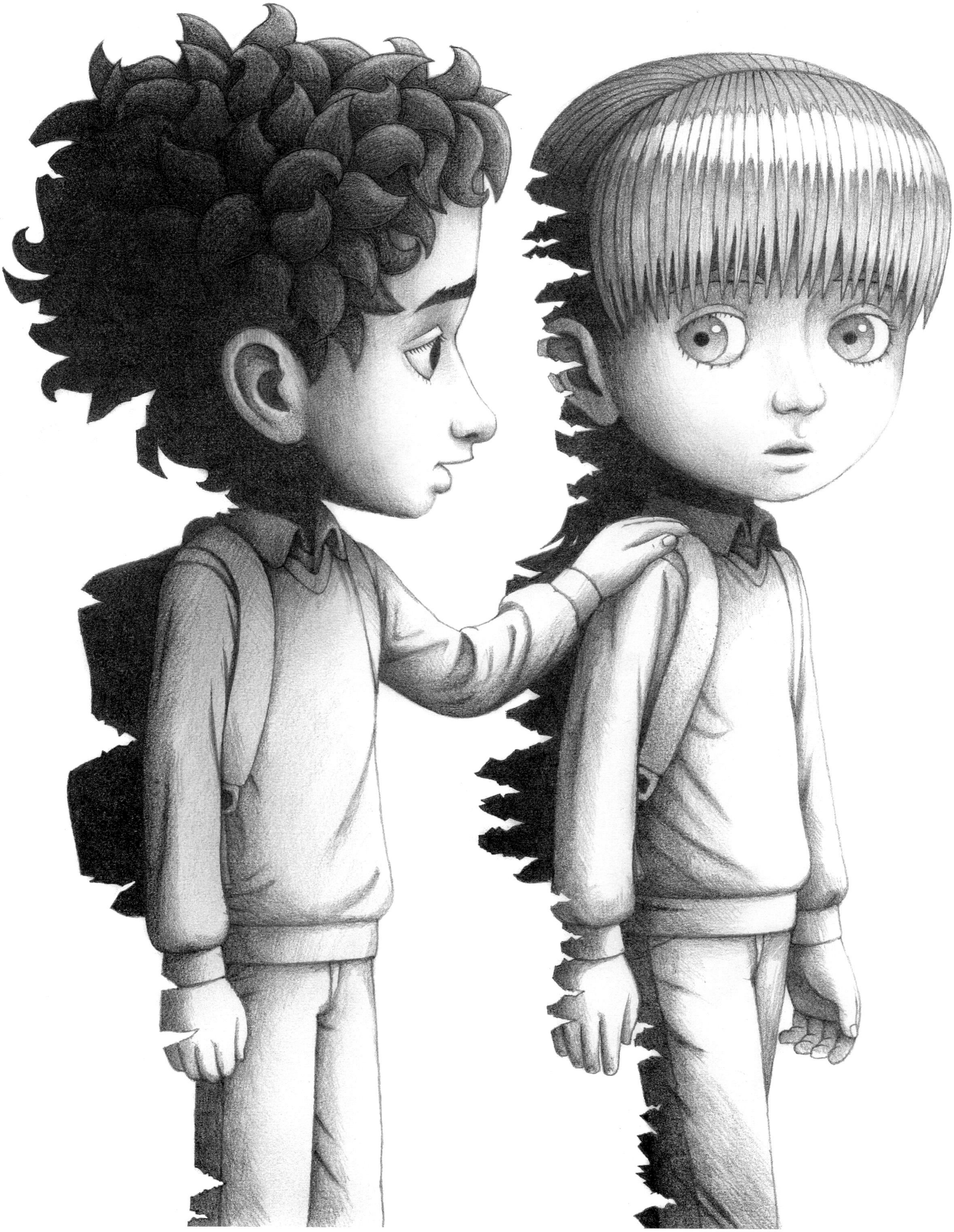

In her book, *Small Things*, without words, Mel Tregonning speaks volumes about childhood anxiety—an issue facing an alarming number of youth today. The tiny demons of worry that surround all children, left unanswered and not confronted, can grow into a debilitating mob gnawing at children's very sense of self, making them feel anxious, alone, and fearful. As Mel artfully depicts, the demons grow in size and number, and cut at the very fabric of young people's being. With their own self-talk becoming more negative, far too often children who are anxious react by retreating from life's adventures in order to escape possible adversity—real or imagined—or they strike back at anyone trying to help them.

Anxious children's blown-up visions of danger and adversity, and their diminished belief in their own ability to cope with and successfully confront these head on, set up a vicious cycle of negativity and dread of failure that feed the demons. When the young boy in the story finds another young person who also has worries and anxieties, in their dialogue, he is able to see that he is not alone in his feelings and that he is capable of shrinking those demons.

The last illustration in the book is a powerful reminder that calling our fears by name and reaching out to others is the beginning of the journey out of debilitating anxiety. It is an important beginning. We as parents and educators can use this powerful picture book as that starting point. We must also help young people develop the skills to confront negative beliefs they have about themselves and to think, call out, and confront their anxious thoughts, so that they can become their own best advocates.

—**Barbara Coloroso**, *author of Kids Are Worth It!*

For more information, visit pajamapress.ca/resource/small_things_extra_content